*On the first day of Christmas
my true love gave to me...*

...strict rules about "playing" his girlfriend. Apparently Ben's mother is driving him crazy, shoving buxom blond brides-to-be under his nose at every turn. I am *no* buxom blonde. In fact, I'm Ben's *un*ideal woman in every way, but he seems to like having me around. And he's not shy when it comes to public displays of affection...for his mother's benefit, of course!

Well, there's something to be said about pretend love—namely, all I want for Christmas is a *real* engagement ring....

Dear Reader,

Christmastime is coming, and even people (like me) who are hopelessly disorganized and never make lists start making them now. What to buy. Who to give it to. What to buy to give to myself (because I really *have* been good this year). I know what I'd *like* to give myself: Ben and Stone, the two heroes our authors have gift-wrapped for you this month. In fact, either one would do.

Take Ben, to start with. The hero of Alexandra Sellers's *A Nice Girl Like You* isn't looking to get married, but he's also not looking to break his matchmaking mother's heart. So when she matches him up with a very nice girl named Sam, he's more than willing to play along. Until one day he discovers that he's gone way beyond playing around and realizes that maybe he's met the woman for him after all.

Then there's Stone, the hero of Jo Ann Algermissen's *A Marry-Me Christmas.* Like so many of the best gifts, he's quite different from what heroine Catherine Jordan originally thinks. Quite different—and much, much better. Turns out her holiday fling shows every sign of turning into happily ever after.

So Happy Holidays to all of you from all of us here at Silhouette, and don't forget to come back next month— next year!—for two more wonderful books about unexpectedly meeting, dating—and marrying!— Mr. Right.

Leslie J. Wainger
Senior Editor and Editorial Coordinator

Please address questions and book requests to:
Silhouette Reader Service
U.S.: 3010 Walden Ave., P.O. Box 1325, Buffalo, NY 14269
Canadian: P.O. Box 609, Fort Erie, Ont. L2A 5X3

ALEXANDRA SELLERS

A Nice Girl Like You

SILHOUETTE YOURS TRULY™

Published by Silhouette Books

America's Publisher of Contemporary Romance

For Louise Jameson,
best of friends,
and
the nicest girl I know

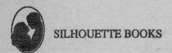 SILHOUETTE BOOKS

ISBN 0-373-52033-6

A NICE GIRL LIKE YOU

Printed in U.S.A.

About the author

ALEXANDRA SELLERS has worked as an actress, editor, insurance saleswoman, legal secretary, palm reader, language teacher and garage mechanic's assistant, among other things, and is an avid student of languages, religion and—as many of her readers will have guessed—Middle Eastern cultures.

She has enjoyed many jobs, but she likes writing best, and it has been her full-time occupation for most of the past fifteen years. "Writing is the next best thing to being independently wealthy," she says.

The idea for this book seemed to come out of nowhere. "But," admits Alexandra, "it may be a result of my own desire to play matchmaker, and a subconscious recognition that, like Miranda, I'm not very good at it in real life. I've never yet put a couple together successfully, though a man did once enliven a party by announcing to a friend, 'Are you the one I'm supposed to marry?' Of course, they never got together. My friend is now happily married (to someone I did *not* introduce her to!) with two children.

"Maybe that's why I'm a writer of romance—it always works out so well on paper!"

Alexandra teaches her own weekend intensive course, "How to Write a Romance Novel," in London several times a year. She loves to hear from readers, who can contact her at P.O. Box 9449, London NW3 2WH, England.

Books by Alexandra Sellers

Silhouette Yours Truly

A Nice Girl Like You

Silhouette Intimate Moments

The Real Man #73
The Male Chauvinist #110
The Old Flame #154
The Best of Friends #348
The Man Next Door #406
A Gentleman and a Scholar #539
The Vagabond #579
Dearest Enemy #635
Roughneck #689

1

Desperate Mother Seeks Nice Girl, Successful, Bright, 20-35, Not Necessarily Attractive, To Play A Part For One Evening Over
Great Home-Cooked Meal. Strictly Legal.

Samantha Jagger set down her coffee cup and
reached into the big china mug in the middle of her
kitchen table. On one side it held a bouquet of slightly
dusty blue artificial flowers. It had been a pretty ac-
companiment to the kitchen's blue woodwork and
cream-and-blue wallpaper when she had first put it
there, but now the flowers stood slightly askew against
the pressure of the various pens and pencils jammed
in on the other side, spoiling the effect a little. Not that
Sam ever noticed, but Justin had remarked once or
twice that a mugful of ballpoint pens wasn't aesthetically pleasing. Whenever he was here, he always
moved it to the windowsill.

"I often need a pen suddenly when I'm sitting at the
table," Sam had told him when he'd complained. "If
I had to go searching through the place for something
to write with all the time, I'd lose my ideas."

"None of them works anyway," Justin had pointed out, meaning the pens, not her ideas. "Don't you forget your ideas when you're scratching around trying to find a pen that has some ink in it?"

There was some justice in that remark, Sam reflected now. The first two pens she pulled out were out of ink, and the pencil she tried next had no point. She could at least stuff the mug with *working* pens, as Justin said, and throw this aged collection into the garbage. She just never seemed to get around to it. The problem was, pens looked so useful even when they weren't, and Sam hated to throw out anything that looked useful. But she would start today, she told herself firmly, by tossing these two dead pens out.

She was luckier on her fourth try, finding a red felt tip that wasn't quite dry, and she circled the ad with an only slightly blotchy oval. Absently tucking all the pens and the pencil back into the cup, she leaned back in her chair, picked up her coffee cup again, and sipped thoughtfully as she reread the now highlighted ad.

It sounded a little phoney. Desperate mothers were usually desperate on behalf of desperate unmarriageable sons or daughters, in Sam's limited experience, and what good would one evening do someone like that? Probably this was a woman hoping that if she could just get her son near a marriageable woman, lightning would strike—the "who knows, anything might happen" principle.

On the other hand, the ad noticeably did not require lack of romantic attachment on the part of the woman. So this interpretation might be all wet. Maybe the woman was desperate over a wild daughter—just to take a guess—and wanted to show her a series of successful role models to try to change her thinking. In that case, there might be a story in it.

Sam specialized in kooky, off-the-wall personal experiences for one of her regular magazine columns, and it didn't take much thought to decide that this was worth investigating. If it was just a woman trying to marry off an unmarriageable son, well, Sam had seen her quota of those—like any reasonably attractive unmarried woman of twenty-five, she figured—and could handle it. And the mother was self-described as desperate, so whatever her problem was, she'd suffered disappointment before. One more wouldn't hurt her that much.

It was a fabulous autumn morning, and Justin would be here any minute, but this would only require a quick note. Sam went to her desk and rooted in a drawer for some decent notepaper she knew she had around somewhere, but all she found was a lined stenopad. She grabbed that and an envelope and returned to the table.

She pulled the red felt-tip pen out of the flower arrangement again and scrawled, "Dear Des Mom: Saw your ad. I love home cooking. Call Sam," and added her phone number. The pen was rapidly drying out, but her number was legible—if you looked closely. When she tore the sheet of paper off the pad, a large corner stayed behind, but it only carried part of the "Dear", and she was already late, so she shoved the torn sheet into the envelope, sealed it and wrote the box number and the newspaper address.

The door buzzer rang, loud and long. Justin, not the mailman. It was one of Justin's few annoying quirks that he always had to announce himself so firmly. Tossing the newspaper onto a chair and leaping up to answer the bell, Sam told herself she wouldn't mind so much if she had a doorbell with a pleasant *cling-clong* instead of this insistent buzzer, which really frazzled your nerves, especially so early in the morning. One day she would have a doorbell with a nice *cling-clong,* because Justin had promised that if the new apartment didn't have one, he would see to it that one was installed.

But of course, if she were living with Justin, he wouldn't have much reason to ring the doorbell, firmly or otherwise. Still, it was kind and thoughtful of him, he was a kind and thoughtful man, and that was why she was pretty sure she loved him.

Sam sometimes did wish that, rather than look to the future when she told him how much she hated her loud buzzer, Justin would take the hint and reduce the duration and impact of his own finger on the button, but he had never quite made the connection between what she said and his own actions. Well, that was her fault. She could have told him more directly. It wasn't that Justin wasn't a sensitive man. He was. Incredibly sensitive, sometimes.

"Hi!" she called into the entryphone. "I'm almost ready. Will you come up?"

"I'll wait in the car," said Justin. Sam made a guilty face. She should have been getting ready instead of dawdling over coffee and the paper like that. Now she still had to put her makeup on, and Justin would sit in the car and fret through every second of the five minutes this would take. Justin hated "impromptitude". At the university he never allowed a latecomer to enter one of his classes, and Sam knew her own tendency to forget the time bothered him. She tried, she really did. The problem was, the world was always throwing interesting things at you just when you should be somewhere else. Like that ad.

"There in a minute," she carolled placatingly, wishing he would come up and have a cup of coffee so she would feel less guilty.

Dashing into the bathroom, she dragged a comb through her tousled hair, snatched up a blue headband that matched her denim shirt and shoved it behind her ears. Her dark hair fell down her back in a cascade of natural curls, but at least it was off her face, and that would have to do. She couldn't spend the time putting it up now, though she probably would have done that if she hadn't wasted her time over the paper. Justin loved her hair, it was what he called "the wild sensuality" of it that had first attracted him to her. That was why he preferred her to wear it in a French braid now in public: he wanted the sensual promise of those black curls kept all for him. Which was very flattering, Sam told him, though she didn't have the patience very often to make a French braid.

Sam smudged on a bit of eyeliner and lots of mascara. Her summer tan was still holding, and that would have to do; she couldn't take time for foundation, either. A little blusher and a slick of lip gloss, and there! Not even five minutes. He wouldn't even be sure she hadn't spent the time waiting for an elevator.

Snatching up her tan cotton jacket, a large battered canvas bag, and her keys, Sam set her alarm, opened the door, stepped outside, and was just closing the door after her when her brain registered her last sight of the apartment, the letter she had written lying on the kitchen table beside her coffee cup. Automatically she shoved the door open again, and dashed across the sitting room and into the kitchen, reaching for the letter.

Clangclangclangclangclang! The alarm went off all around her ears with a noise like the end of the world. Sam shrieked a surprised curse and dashed for the alarm pad, punching in her code.

The clanging went on relentlessly. Of course she knew better than to go back within range of the movement detectors once she'd set the alarm, and of course the code wouldn't work once the intruder alarm had gone off! When the phone rang, Sam snatched it up with relief.

"Bedlam!" she shouted into the receiver. "Bedlam! What's the code? I'm in a hurry!"

"I believe it," said a deep female voice dryly.

Sam recognized the voice. "Phil!" she exclaimed. One of the editors she free-lanced for. "Gee, sorry, but can I call you back? The alarm people will be sending out the cops."

She didn't wait for a reply, but banged the receiver down. Immediately it rang again, thank God, and she scrabbled it to her ear.

"This is Ace Alarm Systems—" a male voice began.

"Yes, yes!" she called, cutting him off. All this was taking so much time, and Justin would be in a lather. "I set it off myself by mistake! Bedlam! Can you give me the number, please? This bell is going to wake the dead!"

And nobody in the building would thank her. Eight-thirty on a Saturday morning wasn't everyone's idea of a good time to wake up, especially not in this building, which was full of artists, actors, down-and-outs and drunks.

"What is the code word, please?" the young voice demanded, self-consciously firm and unflappable.

"Bedlam! I just told you! Bedlam!"

"Oh, right! Oh, I didn't realize...yes, that is the correct code. Are you standing by your alarm activator?"

He was clearly reading from a cue card; he was going to go through the entire ritual with her. Sam rolled her eyes and resigned herself to the inevitable. "Yes, I'm standing by my alarm activator," she said drily.

"Good. Now, I am going to give you a sequence of numbers to code into your alarm activator. Please code them in as I speak. Do you understand these instructions?"

Clangclangclangclang. "Yes, dammit, I understand. Go ahead."

"Are you in position and ready for me to commence with the coded number sequence?"

She was getting a new alarm company first thing Monday morning. Thick but thorough wasn't what you wanted when you had the siren from hell beating in your ears.

"Just give me the code, okay?"

"Are you ready for me to commence with—"

"Yes, I'm ready for you to commence with the coded number sequence! Can you commence already?"

"Certainly, madam." Now she had hurt his feelings. "Please press zero, one, six..."

"Sam? Are you in there?" A loud, firm knocking accompanied the voice on the other side of the door. "Sam?"

"...five, three, three..."

"One second, please!" she called to the door, madly pushing numbers.

"You want me to stop the coded sequence?"

"No, not you! There's a neighbour at the door! Oh, hell! Did I push one three or two? Hold on a sec, I've lost my place anyway." Sam stretched out the full extent of the phone cord and bent awkwardly to open the door. "Hi, Marie! Sorry about this! I'm just getting the code to shut the damned thing off. Yes, can you begin that again?"

"I can't begin again with the same code if you have already entered some of the coded sequence into your alarm activator. Have you done so?"

"Yes, yes, I put in the first few. I got lost at the two threes."

Marie, making an agonized face at the noise, stepped inside and shut the door. She was wearing a pink woolly bathrobe and was barefoot, her pale brown hair tousled wispily around her head. She looked a malnourished thirteen. In one hand she carried a huge kitchen knife.

"In that case, I will have to begin again with a different coded number sequence. Are you ready?"

Sam opened her eyes wide when she saw the knife but said nothing for fear of disturbing the order of the coded sequence again. "Yes, I'm ready."

"Thank you. Please press zero, zero, one, five, one, six . . ."

The sequence was at least twenty-five digits long, probably some kind of protection against anyone's being able to memorize the day's code and then running around breaking into all the places serviced by Ace Alarms, Sam thought crazily, but at least there was silence as soon as she had pressed the last digit.

With a sigh of relief she thanked Thick but Thorough, hung up and turned to Marie.

"What on earth were you going to do with that?" she demanded. Marie was a model in the new waif style, tiny, startled and vulnerable. She was all big eyes and frail bones. The realization that she had envisaged challenging a criminal with a kitchen knife staggered Sam.

Marie shrugged and laughed. "I don't know. Threaten somebody, maybe. I thought maybe you were in here with some... burglar, you know."

"Oh, Marie!" Sam just didn't know what to say. "Thanks. Thanks a lot."

"That's all right. What are neighbours for?"

Sam liked the sound of the old-fashioned, comforting word. Not a word people used in the city much, or at least not with the glow of meaning that Marie's voice invested it with. "That depends how big they are," Sam said sternly. "If they weigh ninety-eight pounds wearing wet socks, neighbours are for staying safely put and calling the police." But if there had been an intruder this morning, she would rather have had tiny Marie next door than some burly six-footer who didn't want to get involved.

Marie only shrugged and set the knife down on Sam's bookcase. "Is that coffee I smell, or are you going out?"

"Justin and I are looking at some places today, but I've got a couple of minutes," Sam lied firmly. "The coffee's fresh."

"You sure? I know he hates to be kept waiting."

She wasn't going to send Marie away coffeeless when she had come to Sam's aid with a butcher knife. Justin would understand. Anyway, it would be nine o'clock soon, and he could listen to the news and the financial update on the car radio. That would take his mind off her lateness.

"He'd be waiting a lot longer if there had been an intruder and you hadn't come to my rescue."

Sam led the way to the kitchen, dropping her jacket and bag and the letter on the sofa en route. Her coffeepot was still hot, mainly because she had forgotten to switch off the hotplate, and she poured two cups.

"There's something wrong with the logic of that, Sam," Marie protested as she followed in her wake. Yawning violently, she sank down into a chair and reached gratefully for the cup she was offered. "But it's too early in the morning to work it out."

"Who cares about logic? It's perfectly true. Cream?" asked Sam. "Sugar?"

"Not this week." Marie made a face. "I've gone up a whole pound since Tuesday. I've got to run miles today as it is. Black's just fine."

Sam liked to keep slim herself, but she was glad she didn't have, or need, Marie's professional obsession about her weight. How could you keep from being a complete neurotic about food if you had to think about your intake of it constantly? Somehow Marie managed, but Sam didn't figure she would be able to. The kind of deprivation Marie put herself through would have had Sam up in the middle of the night stuffing herself with butter tarts in reaction.

"So, you're looking at apartments today? Are you and Justin really going to move in together? That's pretty neat."

"Well, we haven't really said it out loud, but he's buying his own place, and he said he's not going to get anywhere I don't like." Justin was cautious. He liked to do things a step at a time, testing the ground. Sam knew he had almost made up his mind to ask her to move in with him—and even that he was leaving his flat in the family mansion and buying a separate place of his own for that very reason—but it was like him to want to think it over just that little bit longer. Sam didn't mind. She would love living with Justin, or being married to him, and making a home for them both, she knew that, but she wanted him to be sure. She wanted to be sure, too. Things could happen to the most secure relationships. She wouldn't have been comfortable if he'd tried to sweep her off her feet.

She hoped they would be able to find a place they both liked. Sam was pretty easy-going, but she didn't like the minimalist style of Justin's current place, which his mother, a very successful interior designer, had decorated. Sometimes she showed it to potential clients, because she was pleased with it and considered it a "signature" work, but in Sam's opinion it was very damn difficult to live in a signature.

The effect of the minimalist design was utterly destroyed by the presence of any of the detritus of normal living. Sam had been at Justin's apartment once when such a showing was on the cards, and Veronica had swooped through from the main wing of the house to cast a preliminary eye over the place.

Sitting on the violently uncomfortable sofa that lazy Sunday afternoon, with the Sunday paper spread out—in the absence of anything resembling a coffee table—on the otherwise naked pale oak floor at the feet of an uncomfortable piece of sculpture depicting Hunger, Sam had been astonished to feel the paper twitched delicately from her hands.

"I'll return this when they've gone," Veronica had said, wrinkling her nose in friendly conspiracy at Sam before disappearing, the newspaper firmly under her arm, to collect the client.

Sam would hate to live in such a home, and Justin had assured her that he didn't like it, either. He really only lived there as a favour to his mother. His own place would be very different.

Their first appointment for a viewing had been for nine o'clock, a fact that Justin gently pointed out to her when Sam arrived at the car at last at five past the hour.

"Sorry, sorry, sorry!" she sang as she opened the passenger door and slid guiltily inside. "Everything's chaos today!"

"Everything's always chaos," said Justin in a tolerantly amused voice. "It's one of the things I love about you." He didn't let on, but she knew he was irritated; he wasn't listening to the news but sitting in silence. Justin had what Sam privately termed his "martyr" moods. He was annoyed at being made to wait, so he made sure he suffered fully.

"I set off the alarm by mistake, and would you believe Marie came to my rescue with a knife, thinking there was an intruder?"

"Very foolish," Justin said, starting the engine and making a quick U-turn. "That sort of thing will get someone hurt. It's never a good idea to challenge an intruder."

"She thought someone was attacking me."

"If someone had been, she would merely have offered him a weapon to use," said Justin.

Sam didn't argue, but grinned at him. Justin was a little out of touch with the real world; she supposed it was because he'd always been surrounded by money. But she found his ivory-tower thinking attractive most of the time. He was so above the ordinary concerns of life. He came from a long line of intellectuals, and taught English and Canadian literature at the University of Toronto, just like his father. He had also written a short novel that had taken the literary elite by storm. *Bleak Future* had been well reviewed in all the top papers and magazines. ''Justin McCourt has sacrificed all to style, and he has chosen wisely, for he is a supreme stylist.'' That was the kind of thing they'd said about him.

He was also unbelievably good-looking. Tall, slim, fine-boned and fair-haired, he had the looks of an aristocrat. Even in the casual tweed jacket and jeans he was wearing today, he looked smooth and rich. People always responded to Justin as though they knew he was wearing two-hundred-dollar loafers. Sometimes it made Sam nervous, because no way could she live up to Justin's style any more than she could to the minimalist apartment, but it didn't bother Justin. He always said Sam had terrific bones and that meant she could carry off anything.

The first apartment on his list was further uptown than Sam's address, on a very smart street. Sam didn't even ask what the price was. No way was her income going to make any dents in the mortgage here. So she bit her tongue and followed the real estate agent through the huge rooms, smiling as Justin and the agent discussed double height ceilings and en suite guest baths and total square footage and the annual fees for the building's upkeep.

She'd honestly had no idea that this was the kind of place he had in mind. There was even a staircase in the massive double-height living room, which led up to a gallery dining room. There was an "office", a "studio", a "housekeeper's suite", two guest bedrooms with "shared ensuite", a children's bedroom, and a master bedroom ensuite bathroom the size of a tennis court.

For the kind of money this place would cost—for a third of the price!—Sam would far, far rather have a house. Something she could make into a real home. But, as Justin had pointed out, that would mean going out a bit, and Justin felt he should be within easy distance of the university's main campus.

This building was within walking distance, but of course he wasn't serious about buying here, Sam knew. He was only politely faking interest for the agent's sake, having got her out here at this hour on a Saturday and then being late as well. Probably he'd misunderstood her description, or maybe, recognizing his name, she was just trying the top of the market first, regardless of Justin's instructions.

She was a young, attractive, success-hungry woman, and she wanted to sell this mammoth piece of elegant living. "Savvy" was her favourite word. All her attention focused on Justin, whom she certainly recognized as old money and lots of it. She understood his desperate concern for privacy, silence and, above all, taste, her attitude said. She shared such concerns, as those who understood the real values of life must. And Justin, it had to be said, was drinking it up.

"How many apartments does the elevator serve?" Justin was asking.

"Six." The agent grimaced delicately in apology and recognition of Justin's unerring savvy: he had put his finger on the weak spot in paradise. Justin was one of *the* McCourts, and her manner told him wealth enhanced his value as a human. "The elevator on this side serves this half of the building—one apartment every two floors except for the fifth and sixth, which have one smaller apartment each." She grimaced again, as though it was a pity these smaller apartments had been allowed to occur on such holy ground.

"Oh, what a pity," Sam interposed. "I hope you won't have any welfare mothers as neighbours, darling."

They both ignored the comment. Not by the flicker of an eyelash did Justin betray his appreciation, and the agent took her lead from him in an assessment so quick Sam had to admire her for it.

"However..." The agent held up a hand to prevent the quick condemnation of this evidence that brushes with potentially unsatisfactory strangers would be inevitable, tripped lightly over to a door, and opened it. "There is space for a private elevator to be installed, and of course the right to make the installation is already established."

The thought of Justin pompously installing a private elevator to protect himself against the necessity to rub shoulders with the seething mob of the other residents in the building nearly caused Sam to lose it. She choked, pressed her lips together and bent her head. But Justin still wasn't letting on.

"I wonder what the outlay would be," he mused.

Of course Ms. Agent had the figures at her fingertips. She flicked through her competently compiled file and twitched the relevant sheet of paper out without hesitation. She came and stood at Justin's shoulder, where her subtle perfume would just reach his nostrils, and the two of them bent their heads over the builder's estimate.

Sam nearly laughed aloud, suddenly understanding. Somewhere along the line this smartly dressed creature had made up her mind to whip Justin right out from under Sam's nose and sell him the apartment for good measure. Such doubleness of purpose wasn't to be found just anywhere. With real appreciation after that, Sam followed the agent's twinkling feet and tinkling voice in and out of rooms and up stairs and stood out of the way to let Justin receive the full impact of those admiring eyes. Meanwhile, she kept a tight rein on her resident imp.

"And now—" the agent said, smiling conspiratorially into Justin's eyes over Sam's head as they stood next to the gallery dining room in a kitchen that looked like a spaceship "—I've saved the best for last! *You* will certainly appreciate this!" Then she took them out through the huge plate glass doors leading from the dining room onto what she called the "fabulous, fabulous roof terrace" and waved one slim, manicured hand as if she had produced it herself.

It was pretty astounding, all right. The apartment took up the entire top floor of the building and half a floor above. The other half was given over to a spectacular roof terrace whose view of the city was only partly spoiled by the skyscraper hotel overshadowing it on the south. At ten o'clock the morning sun was catching one corner of the terrace, and the agent was careful to lead them to that spot.

"Lovely to have the sun in the morning!" the agent said, in rich but delicately suppressed sensual enjoyment, swinging her head with casual expertise to look out over the view of the city, as though unaware that the sun on her fair, smooth hair made it glow.

"Does it get sun at any other time?" Sam asked innocently.

The woman looked at her, far too savvy to ignore a direct question as to the merits of the place. That might cause Justin to notice what was going on between the two women. "Less in winter, of course. The trees, as you see," she went on quickly, "have been left by the current owner. They are included in the purchase price."

"Ten floors is a long way to go to collect tennis balls," Sam observed, looking over the edge.

The agent, whom Justin was by now calling "Deborah" at her own insistence, chuckled mirthlessly but tolerantly at Sam, as if humouring a slow, too-eager child, flicked a glance at Justin and away, and went on smiling gently to herself for a moment before getting serious again. She turned to Justin. "Now, Justin—" at Justin's insistence she was calling him Justin "—you're savvy enough to know this won't last long on the market. I know I don't have to tell *you* that."

Sam bit her lip and held her imp in severe check.

"The market *is* depressed at the moment, but not at the higher end. We naturally are exclusive agents, and there's no offer in at the moment, but I can tell you honestly, that state of affairs won't last. This one is going to go." She smiled again, holding up her hands, in her own small way an oracle. "I can smell it. So, if you're interested—I don't put pressure on people and I won't be calling you, but—I do advise you, if you *are* interested . . . well, I'll put it bluntly." She could, of course, with a man like Justin, her manner said. "Get an offer in if you're serious." Coy, flirtatious, rather rueful grimace. "Don't say I didn't warn you. I wouldn't with everybody, but I can tell that you like this space. You like it a lot. And it likes you, too, if you'll forgive me saying so."

Sam's imp was getting tired of the muzzle. "And not just the place," she said brightly.

The agent snapped her a look. "I'd kind of like to see you and this space get together," she went on gushingly to Justin. "Frankly I think you were made for each other."

"I bet you only say that when you really mean it, too," said Sam.

Justin was gazing out at the view, pretending not to be affected, but Sam could see the truth behind the casual nod and the flat-toned, "Yes, I'll certainly give it serious thought."

Oh well, she supposed that was just men. Flattery from an attractive woman was mother's milk to men. They drank it in without passing it under the scrutiny of the intellect. Sam wondered if she should be jealous. But she respected Justin too much to think he was anything more than momentarily diverted by the agent's outrageous ego-stroking stock-in-trade. It must work on most people, after all, or such techniques wouldn't have been developed.

In the terribly public elevator there were more discreet threats not to phone Justin, not to pressure him in any way, unless of course Deborah got the offer she was confidently expecting within the next very short period, because she knew he was a man who liked to make up his own mind and who was certainly capable of appreciating both the unusual style and class of a place like this one, and his luck in having it come on the market just as he was looking.

"It's come on the market unexpectedly," Deborah said as they arrived at the ground. "One of the smaller Arab ambassadors was expected to renew his tenancy, and when he didn't, they decided to sell. The market is really ready to boom for places this size, but I advised them to go for it rather than wait. It's not the sort of place everybody is capable of appreciating, but those who do know how to move fast when it's necessary."

Sam was itching to get away. She didn't have much fellow-feeling for the agent, but she was, after all, a woman who was trying to earn a living, and it was a little unfair of Justin to let her think she might make a sale here.

They got away from her at last, since she had another appointment she must fly to. Of course she would ring Justin the moment she felt she had anything else that might interest him.

Out in the street, Sam breathed deeply of air uncloyed by flattery and said with exaggerated relief, "Give me car exhaust any day!"

"Pardon?" said Justin absently. He was looking up at the building's exterior in an assessing way.

"A little too free a hand with the exterior brass trim, perhaps," he confided to Sam. "A little too much on the *nouveau* side. But I suppose one could live with that. The apartment itself has excellent proportions. What do you think?"

"I'm just very glad I'm not one of the smaller Arab ambassadors," Sam said drily.

He smiled bemusedly at her. "Darling, what are you talking about? I'm asking if you like it."

She looked at him. "What do you mean?"

"I suppose there was a certain amount of real estate puffery in what she said, but it's probably true enough that the place could go suddenly. I wonder if Veronica would have the time to come and look at it today."

"Justin, are you seriously thinking of buying an apartment with a bathroom the size of a hockey rink?" she demanded, an incredulous smile beginning to curl the corners of her mouth.

"Darling, you're exaggerating. What about that wonderful terrace?"

"It's a marvellous terrace, Justin, but what do you need it for? What will you do with it besides impress people now and again?"

"Don't be silly, darling. I have no intention of impressing people with it. But it would be quite something for entertaining, wouldn't it?"

This was so unbelievable she had to laugh. "Yeah, if you have ambitions to entertain the entire population of Prince Edward Island at once! I can't believe you're serious."

"Think of it in terms of investment. Deborah's right—the upper end of the market is moving. And places like this will always appreciate in the end. There's always wealth in the world," Justin said comfortably.

2

'May I speak to Sam, please?'' It was a pleasant voice, chesty rather than nasal, with some mysteriously transmitted hint that the speaker had a sense of humour. Not a voice she recognized.

"You got her. What can I do for you?"

A little laugh. "Oh, you *are* a girl! I was a little worried, with a name like that, that it might just be a joke. You're the only reply I got."

"Is this by any chance Desperate Mother?"

More of a laugh. "Yes, it is, and you're quick, too," said the voice admiringly. "I bet I won't have any trouble explaining to you what it is I want to do."

Sam was almost unconsciously drawing a stenopad towards herself across the desk. "What do you want to do?"

"I want to run a scam on my son. Now, don't hang up! Completely legal, and entirely for his own good. Do you think we could meet somewhere? There's a fair bit of explaining to do, and…well, could we meet? I'd be quite happy to buy you lunch."

Sam doodled for a moment on the pad. It was beginning to sound as if her first guess had been right: Des Mom just wanted to set up an unmarriageable son. If so, a little lie now would save them both a lot of trouble. "Ah . . . could you tell me a bit about it first? The thing is, you know, I'm engaged to be married, so if it's wife material you're looking for . . ."

"It doesn't matter that you're engaged, as long as you'd be willing to take your ring off just for one evening. That is, if you have one. Do fiancés buy engagement rings these days?"

Sam decided not to give a direct answer to that. "I don't mind the naked finger look, as long as it won't cause trouble later."

"No, no, nothing like that! I promise you, I'm not trying to trick you into marrying my son! I'm trying to trick my son into marrying someone else. You're the decoy, that's all. Or maybe I mean the ringer."

Suddenly it was starting to sound good. Absently Sam scrawled *Decoy* on the pad. "Okay," she said. "Where and when shall we meet?"

"I don't suppose by any lucky chance you'd be free on Monday night, for dinner?"

Sam didn't have to check her calendar for that. She would have remembered a Monday night date. "Yeah, sure. Is that the big night?"

"Well, otherwise any Sunday night will really do, but Monday would be best. Your fiancé won't mind?"

"No, he'll be all right." If she'd said Sunday Sam might have checked with Justin first, but he certainly didn't expect prior rights over Mondays.

"Hmm. Well, perhaps you're seeing him Sunday, are you?" Before Sam could puzzle this out, she went on, "In that case, we'd better meet as soon as possible. When are you free for lunch?"

"Anytime."

There was a pause. "You're not—unemployed, are you, Sam?" enquired Desperate Mother.

Sam grinned. "No, I'm a free-lance writer."

"Oh, that's nice. That's very nice. Yes, that makes it even better, because that's just the sort of person I *would*...never mind, I'm just confusing you. Now, where are you?"

"I'm on Brunswick, near College."

"Oh, yes, I lived on Brunswick once, years ago, of course. It's a very lively area, isn't it? Is that little Italian café still there on the corner of College and Dean?"

"Yup," said Sam. "Well, sort of. That's where I hang out, in fact. But it's Middle Eastern now."

"Fine. I'm very fond of Middle Eastern snacks. Shall we meet for lunch? Today? Or tomorrow?"

Sam's curiosity was now of cat proportions. "Today. One o'clock all right?"

"Perfect. See you there. Oh—my name's Miranda. Everybody calls me Andy."

It was a beautiful October day, with a clear sky and bright sun, and Sam enjoyed the walk through the fallen leaves down to College Street and along to the little café. Autumn was so fresh, so full of promised beginnings. Maybe it was because the new school year began in autumn—maybe she was just programmed with this feeling she had now that something new and amazing was going to happen in her life. She kicked through the dry leaves, walking slowly, enjoying the scents of fall, forgetting the time and even her appointment in her pleasure in the day.

It was a mild day, and she was wearing only a light summer jacket, butter yellow, which seemed to match the day, her soft red shirt and blue jeans pulled in at the waist with a fat leather belt. Her hair was all around her shoulders, because when she wasn't with Justin she preferred to wear it loose, and she felt curiously easy and free, as if in this moment she had only to think of whatever she most wanted in the world, and the universe would give it to her.

Superstitiously she did ask, just in case what she felt was some angel hovering near, waiting. *Love,* she said to the angel, thinking of Justin's face and smiling at the thought. Of course she knew she loved Justin, but—*I'd really like to* feel *love, to know there's nobody else in the world for me...*

She was late, but there was no one looking like a mother with a taste for arranging events in the life of a grown son in the café, so Sam ordered a coffee and sat down at an empty table. She picked up a badly printed folded single broadsheet called *New Age News* and glanced through it idly while she waited.

"Wanted: sensitive, responsible woman, 25-40, to share small house with similar in the Beaches. Own room, share kitchen, bath. Must Be Psychic," she read. Sam smiled and shook her head. "Home sought for two adorable..."

"Are you Sam?"

She dropped the paper and looked up smiling. "I am," she said to the woman standing over her. "Are you Miranda?"

"But you're *very* attractive! Not Ben's type, but quite lovely! In fact...oh, this is better and better! Tell me, what can I get you? You haven't ordered yet? So sorry I'm late."

"That's all right," said Sam. "I was late myself."

"It's my eldest son," said Miranda. "Ben. He's a very nice man, don't get me wrong, he's just...

different. Impatient of restraint, I call it, when I'm feeling charitable. When I'm not...well. Now, the others are all married, all except Jude, and he was a late baby and is only eighteen. But of my first four, three just did the regular thing and settled down in their twenties and started making a family. But not Ben."

"How old is Ben?" asked Sam, talking around a mouthful of Imam Bayaldi so delicious it was to die for, never mind faint.

"He's thirty. Coming up for thirty-one. Now, Sam—you don't mind my calling you Sam?—I hope I'm not pushy, but take a look at it. Thirty-one means you're forty-five with teenagers, and you can take it from me that's not easy. Thirty-five means you're fifty. Forty means sixty-five."

"Fifty-five," amended Sam.

"Oh, right! Fifty-five. And seventy-five before your first grandchild. I mean, that's no good, it's just no good. Did you say you're engaged?"

"I did."

"Is he a nice man?"

"Very nice." She smiled.

"Well, good. Now, don't you be resisting that trip to the altar for the sake of feminist ideas or anything like that. You get your babies born early, it's a lot more fun than you're imagining right now. It's the best thing there is in life, for a woman or a man, take it from me."

Sam grinned. "Aw, Mom, give me a few years."

Miranda laughed. "Yes, all right, I take your point, but the fact is that women have complete choice over whether to have children or not now, for the first time in history, and like most new technology, we're not really equipped to deal with it. We're not evolving as fast as our tools, and that includes the pill.''

Sam chewed. "That's really original. I've never heard it put like that before.''

"Well, I've been doing a lot of thinking, and I've marshalled a few arguments. Ben thinks they're original, too, but he still doesn't take the hint.''

"Hint?" queried Sam, with a raised eyebrow. It sounded more like a bludgeon over the head to her.

"Yes, I've been too obvious about it, that's been the problem," said Miranda, with disarming astuteness. "And the truth is, Ben's a mule." She made a self-deprecating face and interjected drily, "Can you tell I'm not feeling charitable anymore? It's just no good hammering at him. He just sinks those heels of his into the sand, and if you're not careful, there you are with a cartful of vegetables rotten before you can get them to market.''

"So who's the carrot?''

Miranda wiped her mouth with her paper napkin and took a sip of coffee. "You are. But not the way you think. I've been waving carrots at Ben for two or three years, but he's so stubborn that now even a carrot makes him dig in. You can't move Ben with carrots.''

Sam looked at her with a friendly smile. "You are sure that it's Ben, and not the carrots, who's the problem here?''

"If you mean, are the women I introduce to Ben attractive to him, of course they are. I know what sort of woman and what sort of looks appeal to him. And anyway, he dates on his own. He does bring women to meet me. Not often, but sometimes, and they're very nice women. I know that in his heart he'd really like to get married, but somehow it just doesn't happen. Ben's very special, very different. He needs someone special, too."

Sam was beginning to get the picture. For "special" read "socially challenged".

Miranda grew confidential. "I've found the right girl for him now, a very beautiful girl, no one could resist her. Judith's lovely. Very attractive and intelligent, successful—she's studying to be a doctor. Just his type physically, though I know better than to introduce Ben to someone who's all beauty and no brains, you know!" She laughed. "Far better all brains and no beauty! Ben's much more likely to respond to brains, it's just the way he is. That's why I specified bright and successful in the ad, because Ben knows I'd never try to interest him in someone who only had her looks to offer."

The picture was getting clearer. Someone special and different who isn't attracted to beautiful women, Sam thought. Either he's gay, or he's so ugly he doesn't stand a chance.

"Is Ben handsome?" she asked, thinking of Justin with a little inner smile.

"Well, you know, character is so much more important than looks, isn't it? That's what I've always told my boys. Jude's very good-looking, they all say he'll have to be a movie star, but no one could really call the other four conventionally handsome. But it didn't stop the other three from getting lovely wives. They're attractive, you know, the boys. Ben's attractive, too, he always has women around, but handsome? Anyway, he's not tall enough to be a real dreamboat, which is what we used to call the kind of guy Ben isn't when I was a teenager."

Right. The picture was getting clearer. A socially, vertically, and aesthetically challenged, mule-stubborn, unmarriageable man ... but the image was still a little incomplete ...

"What does Ben do for a living?"

"He takes pictures, mostly."

"Pictures of what?"

"Well, of people. He told me once he liked recording people in moments of change, life changes—'rites of passage', he calls it. He's really very good, and quite successful. People are always asking for him."

She had him now. Perfect. A socially, vertically, and aesthetically challenged, stubborn, unmarriageable *wedding photographer.*

"Does he shoot them through nylon?" she asked, absently.

"Pardon me, Sam?"

"Does Ben smear Vaseline on his lens when he takes pictures? You know, to give them that romantic, misty look?"

Miranda looked shocked. "Oh, no! Oh, quite the opposite! Ben's pictures are always very sharp, very clear. The only time they're blurred is when someone moves as he shoots. I asked him about that once, but he says sometimes movement says something and it may be worth the price of a blurred photograph."

"I think I get the picture," said Sam.

Miranda brought back their filled coffee cups from the counter and settled comfortably again.

"You see, I've introduced him to women before, but I really think that Judith is the one. And I'm determined things won't go wrong because of Ben's stubbornness this time. So I'm not even going to tell him about her. I'm not going to say a word."

"You're not?"

"Not a word."

Sam frowned. "What are you going to do?"

"I'm going to tell him about you."

"Ahh," said Sam. "I see light."

Miranda nodded. "You and Judith must both come to dinner on Monday. You're sure Monday is all right? Because if it would annoy your fiancé, we can put it off. I wouldn't want to spoil things by having you discover suddenly that you can't come at the last moment."

"I won't do that, I promise."

"What about your own family?"

Weird *non sequitur,* but there was no doubt Miranda was family-mad. "I have no family around here. My parents and the grandparents who raised us are dead, and my brother's building bridges somewhere."

Miranda's face went still with unhappy shock. Then she covered Sam's hand with her own. "Oh, my dear. I'm so sorry!"

Just like that, Sam got a lump in her throat. "Yeah, well . . ." she said.

"Oh, I'm so glad you'll be with us on Monday! But why isn't your fiancé—well, never mind, not my business. But you will be there? I want you to come now, even if Ben doesn't."

Sam grinned, recovering. "I'll be there. You go ahead and make your arrangements with Judith. What happens then?"

"Well, I tell Ben all about you. I say I've met this lovely woman who's a free-lance journalist. I'll say he should appreciate that, being in the field himself, you know, people in the arts understand each other, don't they? And I won't mention Judith at all, except maybe to say that I understand that Ella, that's Matt's wife, is bringing a friend who's just moved to Toronto from Vancouver. Because she has nowhere else to go, you know. We've had her for dinner once when Ben wasn't there. It's true she's a friend of Ella's, but it just so happens she's also the daughter of a very old friend of mine. Vancouver's really a very small place, you know," Miranda added parenthetically.

"And what do I do?"

"Well, I'll put Ben in between you and Judith, you see, with him thinking the one he's supposed to be interested in is you. Naturally he'll ignore you and start to talk to Judith."

For stubborn read *completely pigheaded,* thought Sam, already annoyed at being ignored by a man she'd never met. No wonder his mother couldn't get him married off. She was glad she wasn't his type. She wondered what Judith looked like.

"And that's all I have to do?"

"Yes, except that if he does talk to you, if you could just pretend to be a little . . . eager, if you know what I mean. Nothing puts Ben off faster than someone who fawns on him. And he doesn't like toadying women or those who try to impress him."

Bigheaded, too. He must shoot them with heart cutouts and trailing roses. Sam was beginning to feel sorry for Judith.

"So if you could just manage to . . . I wouldn't want you to overdo it, Sam, he's not stupid, he knows I wouldn't invite someone really... just look at him as though you admire him tremendously without knowing very much about what he does. You know, some girls just want money in a man, and some just want a man to be...successful, you know. And some women, even in this day and age, just want a husband. They don't care about the man at all. That's the sort of thing that Ben hates. If you could just contrive to be like that..."

"I promise I'll stare at him with my little gold-digger's heart in my eyes all night long," said Sam.

Miranda laughed delightedly. "Oh, you are a dear! I almost wish—well, never mind! Judith's the perfect girl."

"Maybe I should try to give him my phone number, too." Sam was getting into the swing of this. She was almost looking forward to it.

"Well, there is one other little thing. I wasn't sure about this, but I can see you can handle it. I'll push Ben to drive you home, and of course he'll find some excuse why he can't do that. Would you mind not bringing your car? I'll pay the taxi fare, and if you could just pretend your car's out of commission or let on that you didn't drive because you wanted to be able to drink yourself under the table without having to drive home..."

Miranda paused, struck by a thought. "Can you act drunk? That might be even better, if you could pretend to be drunk—or even get drunk, dear. I don't mind, as long as you don't tell Ben about this in the *veritas* of the *vino* ... then I could forbid you to drive in your condition and ask Ben...well, whatever you'd be most comfortable with."

"I don't think I'd like to fake a drunk," said Sam. "I'll come in a cab and say my muffler needs fixing."

Miranda smiled approvingly. "That's excellent! You're a real conspirator!"

"I don't get it, though. What's the point of him refusing to drive me home?"

"Ah, well, you see, Judith lives close to Ben's place. After you've left in the taxi, Ella will get a call from a neighbour with a problem, and she and Matt will have to leave immediately. Now, they live in quite the opposite direction to Judith, so they'll be in too much of a lather to drive her home. So then I'll ask Ben to."

"But if he's stubborn, won't he refuse?"

Miranda smiled. "No, don't you see? For a start, he's got no idea it's Judith I've set him up with. And secondly, he'll have used up his stubbornness for the night refusing to drive you home. You see what I mean?"

Only through a glass darkly. "Is everybody in on this, then?" Sam asked faintly. "Ella and Matt and Judith and the neighbour?"

"Just Ella and me. And you, of course. Not even Alice and Carol, my other two daughters-in-law. Carol especially, because she'd tell Luke, and Luke for sure would tell Ben. And it wouldn't do to have Judith in on it. She's very eager to meet Ben, of course, but I don't want her acting with Ben as if she's got his mother's and sister-in-law's blessing! That would kill it stone dead, with or without you. No, Ella will just ask her neighbour—they're friends, you know—to be sure to phone her at our number at about midnight, and she'll do the rest." Miranda blinked once or twice. "Now, have I covered everything? Oh—of course this means you should say you have to go and ask to call a cab about quarter to midnight. I'll take it from there. Of course I'll press you to stay a bit longer, but..."

"But my sick cat frets if I leave him for too long."

Miranda laughed again. She had a deep, attractive laugh. Just for a flicker Sam thought she wouldn't mind being interviewed as a prospective daughter-in-law by such a mother, but then she remembered poor old multiply challenged pigheaded Ben who couldn't even take wedding photographs without blurring them. What a pity all Miranda's other sons were already taken, except for Hollywood-handsome eighteen-year-old Jude.

Miranda reached across the table and patted her hand again. "I can see we're going to act very well together. I can't wait for our performance. I almost wish you weren't the decoy but the real thing."

Sam laughed, feeling the warmth of the older woman's liking. "I was just thinking myself I might wait for Jude," she said.

3

"Ben? It's your mother."

"Hi, Mom."

"How have you been?"

"Since last Sunday dinner? Well, pretty good, considering I haven't found Miss Right and settled down into marital bliss since then. Who is it this time, Mom?"

Miranda suddenly felt an obstruction in her throat and coughed to clear it. "What do you mean, darling?"

"Mom, you have a voice that's honey over ice when you want something. Now, we both know what you want from me, so who is it and when do I have to turn up to be given the once-over?"

He was laughing at her, she knew. Ben always said that in view of her own wild sixties life it was so charmingly inconsistent of her to want all her children conventionally married, he couldn't get irritated. Miranda just amused her son, which was particularly galling. But this time she had his number.

"A very, very nice girl, Ben. Her name's Ju—" she coughed quickly. "Jagger. Her name's Sam Jagger."

"Ben and Sam. I like it. It has a certain *je ne sais quoi,* doesn't it? Yeah, I can live with that. You know, Mom, something tells me this time you've hit paydirt. How fast can your friend Harold get the invitations printed?"

"Ben, you're laughing at me. She's really a lovely girl, very different and unusual, and I do want you to meet her. She's coming to dinner on Monday."

"And I guess that means I am, too, huh?"

"Ben, you've already promised to come to dinner on Monday," Miranda said, in some alarm. Suddenly she was a little nervous of her eldest son. There was a tone in his voice she'd never heard before, not when he was speaking to her. As though the prospect of meeting another total stranger as potential wife completely exasperated him. "It's Thanksgiving! You will come, won't you?" No one knew better than Miranda that if Ben seriously wanted to get out of something he would. And he wouldn't trouble to say he had an assignment in Bosnia Herzogovina. He'd just say no.

He sighed. "Mom, I'll come, but just once I'd like to sit down to a meal with my family without you counting your grandchildren and then eyeballing me like a starving peasant looking at a cruel baron, okay? And I'd particularly like it if this little scene did not take place under the eyes of a strange woman who can't stand me on sight."

"That's not true and you know it," Miranda said, taking him up on the easy bit. "Women always like you. It's you who don't like them."

"Well, then, maybe you'll just have to leave me to make my own choice."

"I did that! I did that for all of 1994! It didn't work!" A shout of rich, involuntary laughter billowed down the line to her ear. "Now, Ben, you're laughing at me again!"

The roar subsided somewhat. "But, Mom, who could resist?"

"She's really a very, very nice girl. A writer. A journalist of some kind. You'll like her." Miranda was pleased not to have to lie at this point, though she would have, if necessary. Of course, that was down to Sam, really—everything she was saying was true. Sam *was* a lovely girl.

His curiosity was mildly stirred. "A journalist? How did you meet her?"

Miranda went white, she could feel it. She'd forgotten to arrange this, though it had been in her mind to discuss it with Sam and come up with something plausible. Her brain dashed wildly at possibilities. "Ah—oh, she came to me for a . . . an interview for a "'Where are they now?'" sort of thing."

"Where are who now?"

"Oh—the uh . . . original Toronto cast of *Hair.* Far out, eh?" Miranda laughed, her heart beating like a stick on a picket fence.

"You just grab 'em wherever they're offered, do you?" Ben asked drily. "How did you pitch me to her?"

This was uncomfortable ground. "Now, Ben, I didn't tell her very much about you, so don't . . . she's not . . . she's very nice, Ben. You'll see. And please stop rolling your eyes heavenwards. I can *hear* you rolling your eyes!"

"Acute as ever, Mom," said Ben.

* * *

There was a message from Justin on her answering machine when Sam returned home. She'd wandered a bit after her lunch with Miranda Harris, just enjoying the day, and then done some shopping. It meant she was behind schedule with Phil's article.

"Just calling to make arrangements for the weekend. I'm out of my office all afternoon, so I'll call you again at six," said Justin's voice.

That suited Sam, who sat down at the computer to work. But she found it hard to concentrate. Her thoughts strayed to this afternoon's meeting, and then to the kind of wedding photographs poor, unmarriageable Ben might take. A heart cut-out surrounding the bride, she decided, too-sharp focus, and a bride who has moved at the critical moment. "But it's Art! It's Truth!" the photographer would insist, when the husband complained that he couldn't see his wife's features.

She was still laughing and staring out the window at the autumn leaves when the phone rang.

"Sam? It's Miranda Harris," said the deep, pleasant voice excitedly. "It's all fixed for Monday. I feel like a real conspirator. Come at about six-thirty, is that all right?"

"That's fine. I'll be there."

"Ella's invited Judith, and I've invited Ben. I made him promise faithfully to come, and then I told him about the nice girl I wanted him to meet." She laughed, infectiously, and Sam laughed, too.

"What did he say?"

"Oh, he rolled his eyes heavenwards, he always does, but he promised to come."

"What if he decides to stay away?"

"He won't do that. Not Ben. Not when he's promised and the whole family will be there. Oh, and that reminds me, Sam, we forgot one thing. How you and I met."

"Ah!" exclaimed Sam. "Dat's a veakness in de case, all right, Boris! I vill need a cahver story."

"I've had to choose it already, so now we're stuck with it. I'm afraid Ben caught me unprepared. I said you'd come to interview me for a 'Where are they now?' piece you were writing on the original Toronto cast of *Hair*. I don't know what kind of thing you write. Can you make that stick?"

"Were you in the original cast of *Hair?*" Sam asked with interest. "What was it like? You took your clothes off onstage, and it was considered very shocking in those days, wasn't it?"

Miranda laughed, infectiously again. "If there was one phrase I never thought I'd hear used to me, it was, 'in those days'. It wasn't much more than twenty-five years ago, Sam!"

"Oh, sorry!" The two women laughed together.

Sam pulled the reviews of the production of Toronto *Hair* out of cyberspace and read enough to get a reasonable background. There wasn't a full cast list in any of the papers, but Miranda Martin was mentioned in one as having a thrilling, cut-glass singing voice. Sam didn't have time for more than that; finding a printed program of the show would take real work, but she supposed what she had would do. She wouldn't be talking to Ben much, anyway, if Judith played her cards properly.

She played around with the newspaper library for a while, reading about the world she had been born into, nearly twenty-six years ago. How different everything seemed, so innocent. Then she moved on, irresistibly whizzing through the years to 1979 and the ugliest headline in the world.

Jet Crash Kills 72, it said. Sam stared at it, remembering how, as a child, she had believed that the "2" was her parents. The "70" was all the others, the parents and children and loved ones of others, but the "2" was Andrew and Donna Jagger, who had been flying to a business conference in the States. Sam and Ezra had gone to stay with friends of their parents across the road for the three days their parents would be away. It was there that they saw the news on television.

They had never slept in their own beds again. They remained with their parents' friends while the house they had lived in all their young lives was packed up, and then they were packed up, too, and sent to live with their grandparents in Toronto, far to the East, a city that seemed cold and inhospitable to anyone used to the easy-going ways of the prairies.

She still had one thousand five hundred words to get out to Phil by ten o'clock Tuesday morning, and this wasn't getting it written. Ruthlessly Sam forced herself to leave cyberspace and returned to her article. She stared with helpless lack of inspiration at the screen for two minutes, and then was saved by the phone.

"Hi," said Justin. "Busy?"

Sam sighed and rubbed at the tension that had suddenly lodged over her right eyebrow. She hadn't noticed it before. "Yeah, a piece of froth for Phil on whether white cotton underwear turns men on."

Justin clucked in sympathy. "Darling, that kind of thing is beneath your notice. Why do you do it?"

She sighed. "It's called paying the rent, Justin. Can we take the argument as read? I'm having enough trouble as it is. It may turn men on, but I can tell you—in strict confidence, you understand—that white cotton underwear is leaving me personally stony cold at the moment."

"I confess my own preference is for black satin. Actually that's what I've called about. I've bought you something pretty for the weekend. Do you want to leave Friday night or Saturday morning?"

Sam took the receiver away from her ear and frowned at it, in a quite unconscious movement. She put it back and said, "Weekend?"

"You haven't forgotten we're flying up to the river for Thanksgiving?"

Sam felt all the blood drain from her head. *"Thanksgiving?"* she repeated faintly. "Is this weekend Thanksgiving?"

"Darling Sam, the second Monday in October. Always has been."

"Omigod. Omigod. I've made a horrible mistake." *Can you come on Monday? Are you sure your fiancé won't mind? Where's your family?* Suddenly it all made sense.

Justin's voice got a little chilly. "Well, I hope nothing that can't be put right. The family is expecting us. It's been arranged since August, Sam."

"Oh, God, oh, God, oh, God," she moaned feebly. "Oh, and I promised so faithfully! Oh, God, Justin!"

"What exactly is the problem?"

Sam stared at the blank screen in front of her, hoping for inspiration. Nothing on God's earth would induce her to tell Justin the truth about what she had arranged. It would sound absolutely crazy to him—it sounded crazy to *her*, after all!—and anyway, it was just inexplicable.

"I've arranged to—and I've got this article to finish—look, Justin, if I go, can I possibly get back home by, say, four o'clock Monday afternoon?"

"*If you go?* Sam, what is this? We have Thanksgiving dinner at one o'clock on Monday. It will scarcely be over by four."

"Five o'clock, then. Can we do it?"

"It'll mean booking the plane twice. We were going to come back early Tuesday morning, if you remember."

She knew he was miffed. His voice was clipped. But she had promised Miranda, and on that promise Miranda had arranged everything. Judith couldn't be disinvited now. Sam couldn't just back out. And no matter what Justin said, she knew his family wouldn't care a toss if Sam didn't turn up this weekend. It wouldn't put anyone out except Justin.

"I know, but I forgot it was this weekend. You could come back early, too, couldn't you? That would make it only one trip."

He argued, of course, but somehow, without really understanding why, Sam for once was adamant. She usually gave in to Justin in any contest of wills; it always seemed to matter more to him than to her, and he was so articulate that he could make her arguments sound feeble. But she just couldn't have lived with herself if she'd let Miranda down.

After all, this might be poor unmarriageable Ben's only chance to get a woman.

The McCourt summer home was on the French River, and it was almost as elegant—in a summer home kind of way—as the house in town. The big difference was that it was comfortable. A huge stone fireplace dominated the sunken floor of the sitting room, surrounded by a semicircle of wide, soft-stuffed sofas and chairs. The kitchen was fully equipped but relatively normal and even old-fashioned, with stove, fridge, dishwasher and cupboards where you expected them to be, and the stove all one piece, the oven below, then the hot plates, and the smoke hood above.

It went without saying that Veronica hadn't designed it. Justin's father had inherited it from his parents a few years earlier, and nothing had so far been done to change it.

But still, Sam never felt really comfortable there. She loved the river, she loved the scents and the peace and the trees and the boat bobbing up and down at the dock... but she wasn't really at home. It wasn't that the McCourts overdressed or were too formal; they all shlepped around much like any Canadian family at the "cottage", lazing on the dock or around the fire. It wasn't even that the conversation was self-consciously intellectual and literary, though it often was—what there was of it.

Perhaps it was just that it reminded Sam of her grandparents' home when she and Ezra had first arrived. Sixteen years ago, now, but a sudden memory—a smell, a taste, a strain of music, this house— could make it seem like only last week.

Her grandparents' home had not really been unwelcoming, just different. Just not the friendly, exuberant chaos she had been used to. There was a place for everything, and everything went in its place.

Whatever it was, the McCourt summer home usually made Sam feel lonely.

In deference to Sam's inexplicable determination to leave early on Monday, the traditional dinner had been moved forward a day, so it was Sunday evening when they sat down to the Thanksgiving meal. Sam could only be grateful. The prospect of having to eat two lots of Thanksgiving turkey with all the fixings on the same day had been a bit daunting, because she had no doubt that Miranda Harris would be serving a massive Thanksgiving dinner on Monday night.

But she needn't have worried. Thanksgiving with the McCourts turned out to be in the McCourt, and not the Canadian, tradition. There was no turkey, nor even a ham. Not so much as a chicken wing. Veronica McCourt believed in minimalism in Thanksgiving dinners as much as in decor.

There was buttered asparagus to start, followed by some kind of whitefish with a little elegant sauce, tiny fried potato balls and a slice of red pepper, grilled and then marinated in oil. A salad of lettuce to follow prepared their palates for cheese and crackers. Coffee and elegantly thin chocolate wafers. Two different wines, of course, and Armagnac to follow.

After the meal, the family sat up playing bridge till all hours. Sam watched the game for a while over Justin's shoulder, but the conversation somehow seemed to exclude her. Anyway, she had had a tiring week, and the article for Phil was still eluding her. She went off to bed shortly before one.

But she didn't fall asleep right away. She lay thinking. Her strongest feeling, here in the midst of Justin's family, was loneliness. If things went as she supposed they would, these people would be *her* family some day. When would she start to feel close to them?

4

→ ←

The room was overwhelmingly full of people and noise and the smell of roasting turkey. It didn't help matters that a huge table extended from the dining room into the sitting room, thereby reducing the available floor space, nor that there were several babies set apparently at random on the carpet, and a couple of toddlers practising the newly learned use of their legs.

"You are a darling to come!" Miranda said, peeling off Sam's coat and tossing it negligently over the newel post, where a small mountain of coats had already formed. "Oh, aren't you looking lovely!" she exclaimed, when she turned around. "Is that velvet?" She put out a hand to touch the flowing, glowing skirt of the dress. "Silk jersey! Beautiful. The red is so lovely with your hair!" She stood watching as Sam adjusted herself in the full-length mirror, twitching the long tight sleeves and the high neck of the dress into place, checking the stops on the gold hoops she wore in her ears, and tossing her loose hair casually back off her forehead and shoulders.

"The place is bedlam, as usual, and Ben hasn't come yet, but do come in and meet the others." Miranda said, when Sam had finished. She bent closer and hissed, "Judith's here! Everything's going to go fabulously!"

A moment later Sam was swallowed up in humanity.

"Oh, there you are, Carol!" Miranda reached through a gap in the crowd and encircled the wrist of a pretty, very pregnant woman whose pre-Raphaelite looks were only enhanced by the acre of pale blond hair streaming down over her shoulders and back, and by her absolute lack of makeup. "This is Sam, the journalist I told you about. Carol's married to Luke, my third."

"Oh, hi! So you're Sam. Andy—Miranda—has been telling us all about you! You're here to meet Ben, right?" Carol said with a twinkle, and Miranda slapped her hand in mock indignation.

"Now, you stop that, Carol, you'll make Sam nervous, and you know very well you'll put Ben off! Sam's just here for Thanksgiving dinner because her brother is away out in Saudi somewhere. Ella, come and meet Sam."

Ella was simply stunning. For a passel of boys who had been billed as virtually unsaleable, they seemed to have done very well for themselves in the looks department, if nothing else. Ella looked like someone right off a Paris catwalk. Tall, voluptuous, full-lipped. *Oh, well,* Sam thought, *perhaps the looks make up for a lack of brains.*

"Ella's just finishing her doctoral dissertation in Russian economics, and then she's going to add to my collection of grandchildren, aren't you, Ella?"

Right. So the looks were not making up for a lack of brains.

"In my own good time, Andy," Ella said, with perfect good humour.

"Oh, you always say that! You kids! You'll drive me into an early grave. Now, I'm not going to introduce you to everyone at once, Sam. You'd just forget everybody's name anyway. You get used to Ella and Carol for a bit, and take the others one at a time. It'll be much nicer that way."

"Andy says you're a journalist? What kind of things do you write?" Ella asked Sam as Miranda disappeared.

Sam grinned ruefully. "Anything I'm asked ... or maybe not. Right now, if you can believe it, I'm trying to put together fifteen hundred words on whether white cotton underwear is sexy to men. It's due tomorrow morning at ten, and I'm hovering at the five-hundred-word mark. It's going to be a long night."

"Is it really?" asked Carol.

"Yeah, I hope Miranda won't mind if I leave a little early." Of course, this fit in exactly with Miranda's plans, but Sam figured an excuse that began to circulate early was more likely to seem credible. And, sadly, it was perfectly true.

"No, I mean, is white cotton—darling, you haven't met Sam yet." Carol turned to slip her arm around a broad back just behind her, and drew a man into the group.

"Sam, meet Luke, my husband. Luke, this is Andy's friend Sam."

"Hi!" said Luke, giving her a friendly grin and a handshake. "Nice to see you."

"Hi," Sam said, blinking up at a guy who was at least six foot three and not bad, not bad at all. Maybe not handsome like Justin—he was a lot more rugged—but certainly *not* aesthetically challenged. Thick sandy blond hair down past his shoulders, smiling blue-grey eyes, a chest like a wall and tree trunks for thighs. He looked like a hockey player, even down to the interestingly broken nose. Sam must have heard wrong. She was sure Miranda had said none of her sons was...

"Sam's a writer, Luke, and just now she's writing an article on whether men find plain white cotton underwear sexy. Do they?" Carol demanded.

"Depends on the guy," said Luke reasonably. He paused a moment, thinking it over as an expert. "Depends on how white, too. It'd pretty much have to be new to be a real turn-on."

"Oh, I like that," Sam said. "The advertisers will, too. It's always a good idea to advise the readers they need to buy things. Do you mind if I steal that?"

Luke grinned. "Nope. Depends a lot on the thighs, of course...and the belly..." He reached out and gently stroked the swell of his wife's belly. "Breasts, too—you know."

He was clearly warming to the subject. They were all laughing by now. "You never told me you liked plain white cotton underwear," Carol accused him.

Luke looked affronted. "There's lots of things I haven't told you about that I like."

"There *are?* Why?"

"Well, think about it! Can't do everything at once, woman! What'll we do if we've used up all my fantasies before we're forty? You haven't told me all yours already, have you?" he added in horror.

Carol's cheeks were by this time a little pink. "Luke, will you—" she began softly, and then turned as the doorbell sounded again.

"That must be Ben!" Miranda appeared from the direction of the kitchen and paused at the sitting room door to give Sam a quick, conspiratorial glance, then moved on down the hall to the front door.

Sam's heart was suddenly beating harder, for no good reason. *Stage fright,* she told herself. *I'm nervous about playing a part.* Ella was saying something, but Sam didn't hear, and she realized with a little shock that she was straining to hear what was going on at the door.

"Ben, how terrific! Hardly late at all," Miranda was saying. "That's not much of a coat! Aren't you cold?"

Deep, pleasant laughter. "It's Thanksgiving, Mom, not Christmas."

"I know, but you're so thin, Ben. Don't you feel the cold?"

"No, I don't feel the cold." From the tone of his voice Sam could tell he was smiling. There was the sound of another addition to the mountain of coats on the newel post, and then Miranda and Ben entered the room.

"Now, Ben, come and meet my friend Sam. I know you're going to like her," said Miranda, and Sam turned.

"Sam, this is Ben," said his mother proudly.

She got a quick impression of darkness: black hair, black eyes, and a kind of intensity of energy that drew the focus of everyone in the room, like a quasar or whatever it was in space that was irresistibly magnetic.

"Hi, Sam," said Ben, putting out his hand.

"Hi," said Sam, slipping her own into it and smiling at him. "I understand you want to get married."

Ben flung his head back with a roar of laughter, and Sam took the opportunity for a good look at him. He was different, all right, especially if Luke was your model. He was slim and wiry, with a rough-hewn nose, a broad forehead, a wide, mobile mouth, and a strong chin, and he sure wasn't as tall as Luke. No more than five-ten, Sam thought drily. He wore a casual shirt and loose, baggy trousers that said he wasn't a man who thought much about clothes. His eyes squeezed shut as he laughed, and the thick black lashes spiked in an attractive curve. There was something very, very familiar about him, and for a minute Sam wondered who he reminded her of.

"Hi, bro," said a voice, and Sam looked up to see another blond giant appear at Ben's left. He wrapped an arm around Ben's shoulders and grinned down at him from his superior height. "Still alive, are you?" Luke went over and hugged him, too, and then a third from the same mould, whom Sam hadn't met, called Simon. Watching them, Sam suddenly understood a great deal. Yes, he was certainly different, Ben, his thin, dark leanness of form and his curious intensity in startling contrast to the open ease of these blue-eyed Titans. And yet he was clearly in some way a pivot, a centre for them all. Within two minutes of his entering the room all his brothers were standing around him.

Sam could feel the draw herself. The dark magnetism electrified her, made her feel more alive, so that she almost unconsciously wanted to stay within the force field. And yet, it wasn't entirely comfortable there. His eyes were too penetrating for that, as if he could see whatever it was you most wanted to hide.

She could readily believe that he didn't use Vaseline on his lens when he took wedding photographs; he wasn't a man to cloak reality for anyone's comfort. His pictures probably were far too revealing for the comfort of most brides and grooms. No heart cut-outs, either, Sam told herself. Probably one look would tell you whether the marriage was going to last or not.

"Oh, Ben, you haven't met Judith yet," Ella said after a few minutes of chat, when a fabulous blonde slipped up to her side with raised eyebrows and shoulders in a "can poor little me join the fun?" posture. Ella put an arm around her friend and drew her firmly but casually into the circle. "Judith, meet Matt's brother Ben."

"I've really, really been looking forward to meeting you," said Judith earnestly. She was wearing blue angora that clung to a body she'd clearly borrowed from a raunchy magazine. Sam didn't think she'd ever seen breasts that big right up close like this. For once she could understand why men stared at breasts. So this was Ben's type, was it? It certainly left Sam out of the running, not that she was interested. "I've heard *so* much about you!"

"Really?" An indescribable look crossed his face, and Sam suddenly remembered that this was supposed to be *her* role, gushing at him. Miranda had told her that women gushed at him, and now she believed it. He was dead sexy—her own temperature had gone up two degrees at a distance of four feet. She wondered absently if he had a reputation for driving a woman crazy in bed. She could believe that without any difficulty. The thought of him turning the intensity of those dark eyes on you with sexual need...and his hands... The skin on Sam's thighs twitched spasmodically.

She was beginning to understand just exactly why Ben wasn't bothering to get married. Miranda had an uphill task here, all right, but not for any of the reasons Sam had imagined. She was sure glad Miranda's target was Judith and not her, because Miranda's poor, multiply challenged, unmarriageable son looked like a heartbreaker.

Just then Ben reached out and slipped an arm around her waist. Sam took a deep breath and tried not to shiver.

"And have you met Sam, my fiancée?" Ben asked Judith, to a chorus of shouted laughter.

They sat down to eat a little after that, twenty adults and assorted infants at a table that ran the length of the dining room and through the arch into the sitting room. Sam by now had been introduced to everyone: Arthur Harris, Ben's father, who was sitting at the far end of the table and was the image of his three middle sons; Simon and Jude, the other two brothers; Simon's wife, Alice; several cousins, uncles and grandparents; the toddlers and babies. There were also two couples who lived in the street. Sam had already forgotten half the names she'd heard.

Miranda, at the opposite end of the table to her husband, had placed Sam on her left, with Ben on Sam's left, and Judith on Ben's other side. Opposite were Carol and Luke. When the turkey and the ham had been carved and passed around, and all the mountains of yam and potatoes and turnips and peas and every other vegetable under the sun had found their way onto everyone's plates, and the gravy boats had been emptied and the table had settled in to eat, a small silence fell at their end of the table, and Sam groped for something gushing to say to Ben that would put him off her forever.

She was acutely aware that Ben had chosen white turkey meat, lots of ham, had used a little gravy on the turkey but butter on his potatoes and yam, had put a spoonful of cranberry sauce exactly where the splash of colour was called for on his plate, and had strong, lean hands that never touched anything without grasping it firmly...except her own wrist. He had brushed that involuntarily when he picked up his knife, and that was when she'd noticed how sure his grasp on everything was, when she found herself wishing he would wrap his fingers around her wrist. That was all she wanted, nothing more—just to feel that certain, secure clasp on her wrist, just to know what it was like. It shouldn't have been all that difficult to find something gushing and awful to say to him, but it was. Sam had never been so tongue-tied in her life.

In that little moment of silence between the chit-chat about the food and the embarking on real table conversation, while Sam was still racking her brain for something to say, Carol leaned across to her brother-in-law and opened the evening with, ''Sam's working on an article for a woman's magazine about whether men find plain white cotton underwear sexy. Do you think they do, Ben?''

He looked at Sam sideways. That was all he did, just look, but the glance was so full of humour, physical awareness and sexual curiosity that Sam caught her breath as if he'd suddenly touched her.

"Who are you writing it for?" he asked, but the eyes, oh, the eyes were saying something very different. Sam restrained herself, with difficulty, from taking the look personally. It was just the way he was, she told herself ruthlessly. He was just a very, very sexual person. A man who liked women.

She groped for her wineglass and swallowed a large mouthful. *"Woman 2 Woman,"* she said. "Fifteen hundred words."

Ben nodded, raising his eyebrows. "That's a lot of words for something like that."

"Yes, and all one thousand five hundred are due at ten tomorrow morning," Sam said feelingly. "I've only had the assignment a week. Someone else fouled up, and the editor called me to produce a last-minute fill-in. I said yes before I realized what a menace it was going to be. It just won't budge."

"So, is it sexy, Ben?" Carol prodded. "Luke says it's all in the thighs, and whether the cotton is white enough."

The conversation had silenced the whole table. "My vote is for colours," said Simon. "Rich colours. White's too virginal."

"Some might consider that a draw," Ben stated lazily, and Sam was left wondering whether he was among their number.

"White's a great contrast on dark skin, though." That was Jude.

"Yes, it's a pity Sara couldn't be here tonight," Miranda said, in what sounded like a *non sequitur* but, judging by the laughter, wasn't, or not entirely. "You'll like her, Sam."

"The thing about white," Judith said simply, "is that any colouring dominates it. Blondes can dominate white." Her own hair was blond, but she said this without any apparent desire to conjure up the image of herself in white underwear in anyone's mind. She wasn't flirting, just contributing her mite.

"Yeah, you're right," Sam said thoughtfully, leaning forward a little to see her past Ben, suddenly remembering what her duty was here. "That's a good point. I can work that in."

"On the other hand, it may be that where underwear is concerned, a man is not exactly looking for a woman to dominate the colour." Ben pointed this out softly. His voice was velvet, and Sam wondered whether it was stroking Judith's skin as delicately and surely as her own. "He may prefer to do that himself."

"Oh, sexist!" a female voice carolled out, while Sam's stomach leapt for a trapeze that was just out of reach and dropped a dizzying distance.

"Not sexist at all," Ben objected lazily. "Just what is. Politics dictating sex is as bad as sex dictating politics."

"I bet it would be easy to come up with fifteen hundred words on why men want to dominate women in bed, wouldn't it?" Ella said to Sam.

"You only get three words out of that." Ben intervened, before she could answer. "Same reason women like to be dominated by men in bed. Because it's sexy. And whether they admit it or not, most women know it."

Her stomach still hadn't hit earth yet, and now it was caught on an updraft. Sam carefully applied herself to a mouthful of turkey. Chewing wasn't easy, but at least it gave her something to do besides gaze at Ben like a hypnotized mouse.

"Okay, but we're getting off the subject here, aren't we?" Carol was nothing if not dogged. Sam wondered what work she did. "Is plain white cotton underwear sexy, and if so, why and to whom?"

"Not plain. There's a little leeway here," Sam explained. "Just white cotton. I can add lace if I need it."

Ben glanced at her. "You don't," he muttered out of the corner of his mouth.

Her stomach gave up trying to land on anything stable and shot off into permanent free fall. The corners of her mouth twitched, but she stared resolutely at her plate.

"I'm saying nothing," she said. And this man had the nerve to complain because women fawned on him? What did he expect, if he treated them like this?

"One thing you can say about underwear," Arthur chipped in from the other end of the table. "And that is, that it's sexier than nudity. But I've never been able to figure out why. If someone could explain that to me, I'd be grateful."

Sam tried to imagine Justin's father saying anything like that, or this conversation taking place around the McCourt table. Imagination failed to conjure it up.

"That's a good one, Dad," one of his sons said. "It *is* true, but why?"

"Why do we wrap Christmas presents?" said Luke.

"But that's not the whole answer, is it? Why is a long skirt with a slit up the thigh sexier than a miniskirt?" Jude asked.

Arthur said, "You boys don't know what you're missing. Miniskirts in the sixties were very sexy. But that was because we'd never seen naked legs before. Now you see everything, even when you'd rather not."

The conversation began to break up into smaller groups after that, and Ben turned to Sam and said, "Speaking of nudity, who are you writing the article on the first *Hair* for?"

She was ready for this. "Oh, I'm just doing that on spec. I thought I'd check around a bit and see what there was, and then offer it to an editor for an anniversary piece."

"Ben was in *Hair* one night," Miranda offered then, overhearing. "I never told you that. That might help sell the idea for you, mightn't it? Gives you something to hook it on."

Sam smiled bemusedly. "He was?" She turned to Ben. "You were?"

"I got tired of waiting for Mom backstage, and whoever was supposed to be looking after me wasn't, I guess. I saw Mom onstage and made for her, and by that time everybody was taking their clothes off. It seemed like a good idea to me, I hated clothes."

Miranda was laughing. "He got his shoes and shirt and jeans off, I remember, but I stopped him before he got to his undershorts. I picked him up and held him while we sang the number. It brought the house down, of course."

"*That's* where you got your taste for the limelight!" Carol said.

"Not at all," Ben said. "I liked it well enough then, I remember waving at all the faces, but that was enough for me. I've never particularly wanted to be on that side of the camera again."

That was when the penny dropped. It was probably the word "camera" that did it. Sam carefully set down her fork and turned to Ben almost in disbelief. Her eyes opened a little wider in shock, and her mouth opened, too, her jaw dropping slowly but inexorably to its fullest extent. "My God!" she exclaimed. She flicked a glance at Miranda, closed her eyes and took a deep breath, then looked at Ben again. "I don't believe I didn't...! You... you're *Ben Harris!*"

It really was the last straw. In addition to being the sexiest thing since Adam, Miranda's aesthetically, socially and vertically challenged, pigheaded, unmarriageable son was the man Canada's top newspaper had just called, "The most disturbing and penetrating war photographer of the whole generation since 1945."

5

'I'm sorry you have to leave early,'' Miranda said.

Sam was sorry, too. She was having a fabulous time. The sitting room didn't seem nearly so crowded now that she knew everyone in it, and of course the table had been removed, too. If it hadn't been for Phil's article, she probably would have scuppered Miranda's plans without a thought and stayed on.

It wasn't just Ben. She liked them all. It had been a long time since she'd been part of such a happy family group. So long that she'd actually been taking the McCourts as her yardstick on how families were. She had even begun to believe that her memories of her own family had been created out of the whole cloth of need, rather than truth.

But it *was* possible for families to be as happy as she remembered. Not perfect, but happy.

''I do have to go,'' she said sadly. ''Phil will be in real trouble if I don't deliver that article.'' The white underwear article was headlined on the front cover, and that couldn't be changed. There simply had to be a story inside. Phil was counting on her.

Everyone understood, but they all seemed genuinely sorry not to have her stay longer.

"Could I call a cab?" Sam asked, suddenly remembering that she'd left the car at home.

"Oh, don't do that! You live so close, someone can run you home. Ben, you wouldn't mind, would you?" It was Miranda who spoke, and with her words, reality burst the little bubble Sam had spent the evening in. She was here under false pretences, not as herself, but as a decoy.

And clearly Miranda didn't like her quite as much as she had made Sam feel—not enough, at any rate, to let her forget her plans to marry Ben off to Judith. A lot of Miranda's interest in her must have been faked, and perhaps the rest of the family was just very polite.

"No, I'll get a cab," Sam said. She just didn't want Ben's rejection added to the subtle pain she now felt.

"I'll drive you," said Ben, getting to his feet. "You're where—on Brunswick? It'll only take ten minutes, and who knows when a taxi will get here?"

She was looking at his mother as he spoke, and she saw a curious mixture of expressions cross Miranda's face: surprise, chagrin, pleasure. She couldn't tell which was uppermost. Not pleasure, she thought. Sam turned to Ben. She wanted to turn his offer down, but he was right—on Thanksgiving, a taxi might not be available immediately, and she had to get down to that article.

"Thanks," she said. "I really do need to get going."

The streets were almost deserted. She sat beside him in silence for a mile or so, watching the reflection of the street lamps bounce off the hood of the car, her thoughts wandering.

Suddenly Ben said, "Why did you accept my mother's invitation tonight?" and she jumped in surprise. She turned to look at him, but he was watching the road.

"I have no family when Ezra's away," she said.

"No, I mean, why did you agree to let her try to set you up with me? You didn't know who I was, so it's not success you're after, and you don't seem to me to be desperate to get married."

She laughed softly. How to answer this without giving Miranda away?

"Are you?"

"Desperate for marriage? No."

"You involved with someone at the moment?"

She glanced at his profile in surprise. He met the look briefly, but his eyes were all darkness. She had an impression of bottomless depths, and was glad when he looked away again to the road. In depths like that, anything could happen to you. You could lose your head, drown ... anything.

"I am, yes. How did you know?"

"Are you fishing for compliments, or what? A woman like you isn't without a man unless she wants to be, and you don't act as though you're off men at the moment."

"Thank you," she said, though the first part certainly wasn't true. "I guess."

He laughed. "So, I ask again, why did you take part in this little charade of my mother's?"

"You think Miranda invited me in an attempt to set us up?"

"I know so. She told me. I was all prepared for another big-breasted blonde. Someone like Judith, for example. Mom must be changing her tactics somewhat."

She gave vent to a little, irrepressible laugh. "*Are* big-breasted blondes your type?"

"I don't have a 'type'. But as long as Mom thinks I do, I always know when she's invited a woman for the purpose of getting me married off. So I let her go on in the fantasy."

"Maybe she's worked that out at last," Sam offered. She felt constantly on the edge of laughter, for no real reason she could pinpoint. Maybe just because her whole being seemed energized in his company.

"Maybe she has, Sam, but you're evading the issue. Why did you come?"

"What makes you think that I knew of Miranda's plans?'she queried.

"The fact that you proposed to me two seconds after I walked in the door shed some light on it," he said drily.

She laughed aloud. "Oh, right, I forgot that!"

"So, why? I know you're avoiding answering, but I'm going to drive around in circles until you do, so you may as well cough it up now."

She just didn't think it would be fair to Miranda to tell the whole truth. After all, Judith might still be a possible candidate, and the truth would certainly put the kibosh on that. So she tried a half-truth.

"Because I like Miranda, and she wanted me to come. And maybe because I liked her so much I figured I wouldn't mind being married to a son of hers just to have her for a mother-in-law." She shrugged. "I don't know."

He flicked her a glance just as the light from a street lamp washed his face. She felt the look pierce her, as though in those few seconds he had seen her soul. "What's the name of the guy you're seeing at the moment?"

"Justin."

"Poor Justin."

That irritated her. "Why do you say that?"

"Because he is not going to keep you, though if he's any kind of man at all, I'm sure he thinks he will. Now, don't waste your energy bridling at that, you're almost home and I've got a proposition to put to you. Can you spare me an extra five minutes from that article?" To her surprise, he was pulling up at the curb near her building. He had come by the back streets, and she hadn't noticed where they were.

"All right," Sam said cautiously, though she was still irritated by that crack about Justin. What made him think he knew how serious she was? How dare he suggest she didn't love Justin?

Ben killed the engine and turned to face her, resting his arm lazily along the steering wheel.

"I'd like to run a scam on my mother, and you're the perfect one to do it with," he said.

Sam gasped so hard she choked and immediately started coughing. At least the coughing covered her uncontrollable laughter. *Oh, great!* she thought. *First help Miranda run a scam on Ben, and now help Ben run one on Miranda. What a lunatic family they are!*

"You're crazy! What sort of scam?" she said, when she could speak.

"I'd like you to come home with me Sunday nights for the next few months, as if we're seeing each other regularly. That's all. You don't have to pretend we're in love, or even that we're sleeping together. If you want to, you can even be clear that we're not."

She looked at him. "Who's going to believe that you're seeing a woman you're not sleeping with?" she asked ironically, before she thought about the import of what she was saying. But he didn't seem to take it on board, which meant he had less sexual ego than most men, Sam supposed.

"It doesn't matter much what anyone believes. As long as I turn up with you, Miranda can't be inviting one of the mammoth-breasted blondes she seems to have an endless supply of, can she? And maybe I can be comfortable with my family again. You don't know what a match-making mother is like."

"No," she said softly in the darkness, thinking she would have liked someone in her life who wanted grandchildren from her. To her complete amazement, he reached out and covered her hand with his.

"Sorry," he said, suddenly remembering that Miranda had told him her parents were dead. "I know I'm lucky, and you weren't. I didn't think."

She had to swallow. "That's all right."

"So, will you do it? Can Justin spare you on Sunday evenings for a while? It doesn't have to be absolutely regular—I can't always make it myself. You could be working flat out on something and not be able to turn up at the last minute. It's the fact of you, not your actual presence, that's going to do the trick."

"But where will this get you?"

"I told you, back to normal family life. I just want to be able to hang out with my family without feeling I'm constantly being assessed as husband material by a strange woman."

"Why don't you just take your own girlfriend home?"

"I'll tell you why. Because my mother starts talking marriage to any woman I bring within ten yards of her kitchen. She's just compulsive. She can't help it, no matter how earnestly I ask her to shut up. The result is, she either scares them off so thoroughly that they find excuses not to speak to me again, or they start planning whether to have a boy or a girl first. It kind of puts a crimp in my style. You can't develop a relationship back end first."

"No, I can see that." She laughed again. "Didn't you ever try warning them before they met your mother?"

He rubbed the back of his neck. "Try warning a woman that your mother is going to talk marriage to her." He shook his head. "That throws it just as far out of whack. They think I'm testing the waters. Take it from me. So, what do you say?"

"This is all strictly within your family? I won't have to confess to Justin one day because the tabloids have run a picture of us and are speculating about the new woman in Ben Harris's life?"

"I'm not that interesting to the gossip writers, but you have a point. This is for the family only."

It occurred to Sam then that if she said no she would probably never see his family again, never have another evening like this one. She had liked them a lot, and she thought they liked her, but it wasn't likely that Miranda would invite her again. Sam might call Ella or Carol, of course, but she wasn't short of woman friends, and she doubted if they were.

Ben would take her into the heart of the family. That was what was missing from her life at the moment; she hadn't realized how much until she had compared the Harrises to the McCourts.

She didn't let herself think that if she said no she wouldn't see Ben again, either.

"Yes," she said, before she could come up with reasons against.

"Good." She noticed that he didn't reconfirm with any phrase like, "You'll do it, then?" "I know you're pushed for time tonight, so I won't keep you any longer, but I'll call you tomorrow, if that's all right."

"That's all right," said Sam, wondering why her heart was beating as if she had just broken the record for swimming Lake Ontario.

"Just one other little thing," said Ben, as his left arm came off the wheel and his right arm came up, and both of them reached for her. She was in his embrace before she knew it, so unexpected was his move; and now her heart was thumping as if she'd just made the return swim, too.

"What are you doing?" she asked, with contemptible feebleness, and then she had to look up into his dark face.

"Miranda will ask me if I've kissed you when I go back," Ben said softly. "And tomorrow, she'll ask you. There's one way to be sure we get our stories straight."

He was smiling as he bent over her, and then his mouth met hers in a sweet, soft kiss that she felt to the tips of her hair. Her heart kicked once, in protest at being overworked, then settled into its rapid, heightened rhythm.

She couldn't be sure whether, in the second before their mouths met, his lips had lost their smile.

* * *

The kiss didn't last very long, or at least, she didn't think it did. Time did funny things sometimes. "Well," he said regretfully, drawing back a little. "What a pity you've got that underwear to think of."

She blinked twice before she remembered. "Yeah," she said. She struggled a little, and he let her go. To cover what seemed to her an awkward moment, she said, "I wish I'd got some brilliant inspiration from your family tonight and could just go up there knowing I was going to dash it off in two hours instead of punch my head against the keyboard all night."

"What's the cover headline?" Ben asked, absently stroking a strand of hair away from her cheek and setting it behind her shoulder while her blood rushed up and down under his touch like a demented mouse. "Do you know exactly?"

"White cotton underwear—do men think it's sexy? Do you?" Sam recited from memory. If she'd done nothing else over the past week, she'd read that headline so often she would probably be able to recite it from the grave.

He shrugged. "Why don't you include men's white cotton underwear and what women think of it? With that headline, there's room for it."

She went still, staring at him. "Yes, yes!" she whispered, as the clouds parted and the light of inspiration struck her at last. She closed her eyes tightly and then opened them again, concentrating as the article began to write itself in her head. It wasn't exactly what Phil had in mind, but at this point she would be grateful for almost any fifteen hundred words of connected prose. "You're brilliant!"

"It's going to work?"

"Seven hundred and fifty words each—that's a piece of cake!" She reached up and kissed his cheek. "Thank you, I must go!"

Her hand found the handle behind her and opened the door, just as Ben's arm involuntarily came up again. He dropped it and watched her go. "Good night," he said softly. "I'll phone you tomorrow."

"Good night," Sam carolled, and then she was gone.

Ben started the car and drove around the corner to the front of the building, watching as Sam dashed up the front walk, her coat flying behind her in the night. Light fell on her as she approached the lobby, shadowing her delicate bone structure at temple and cheek, a glow on her black curls. He watched till she had unlocked the inner door and gone through and disappeared out of sight, and still he didn't move his foot from the brake.

"What the hell am I doing?" he asked the night. He was usually clear about his actions, but not this time. It was perfectly true that he wanted to spike Miranda's guns and had been searching for a solution for a while, but he knew damn well there was something else going on. Something that was leading him, rather than him leading it. But he didn't know what it was.

You got hard the second you kissed her and it hasn't worn off yet, Ben told himself ruthlessly. You think there might be a clue in that?

"That was a fabulous meal last night," Sam told Miranda. "I haven't enjoyed myself so much for ages. And the food was just delicious!"

"Oh, I'm so glad you enjoyed yourself. They're a nice bunch, aren't they, my boys?"

"Why did you tell me Ben was a wedding photographer? Why didn't you tell me who he was?"

Miranda went off in a peal of laughter. "Is that what you thought? I *certainly* never told you so! The thing is, I tend to forget how well-known he is. He's just Ben to me, you know?"

"Yeah, I see," Sam said, liking the sound of that.

"You liked him, didn't you?"

"I'm saying nothing," said Sam firmly.

"Did he kiss you good-night?"

"I'm saying nothing." Her stomach did a little backflip at the memory, just to remind her it was there.

Miranda giggled. "Oh, isn't it fabulous that all that planning should... you know, last night I *completely* forgot the whole plot. I was so glad to see how much Ben liked you that I just forgot you were there as a decoy. So when you had to go home, of course I thought it would be a good idea if he drove you...and then I suddenly remembered the whole thing! You know, I promised myself I'd never again press Ben to take home a girl I thought he liked, but I just...I can't control myself somehow. I was so angry with myself, because I thought he'd say no, the way he always does, but he didn't, did he? He did kiss you good-night, didn't he?"

Sam was beginning to see justice in Ben's complaints. This kind of thing might easily drive a woman away, even from Ben. Conversely, it might make you think Ben was head over kneecaps in love with you and you could safely ditch all your other men.

"I guess you've forgotten I'm already engaged," Sam said firmly.

"Oh, damn, I've offended you, haven't I?" Miranda said engagingly. "I really just can't stop, no matter how much I promise myself. What's your fiancé's name again?"

"Justin." And just in case Miranda suspected she'd pulled the name out of the air, Sam added, "Justin McCourt."

"Oh, my, you're dating the McCourt son? That's interesting. I dated Hal for a while, years ago, before he gave up and settled down with Veronica. Ah, well, every girl has to do it, I guess."

"Do what?" Sam knew she shouldn't get sucked into this conversation, but the question was involuntary.

"Flirt with the idea of marrying real wealth. But you're too alive for that bunch, Sam, take it from me. They'll have your heart pumping embalming fluid inside a couple of years. That's no life for you."

Sam took a deep breath. "Miranda . . ." she began.

"Oh, I know, I'm sorry! Let's change the subject. Did you get your article written last night?"

"Yes, thanks, I did."

"That's good. Are you free on Sunday, Sam? Would you like to come to us for dinner again?"

She was incorrigible. She really was.

"Miranda," said Sam sternly, "what are you going to do when Ben bites the dirt and you've got them all married off?"

"Start on the rest of the world," said Miranda. "There are lots of lonely people out there, you know."

"Hi."

"Hi," Sam replied softly. There was something

very, very irresistible about the intimacy of the exchange of greetings, and she was already smiling.

"So, you wanna get married?" Pure seduction, the soft invitation to laugh, or...

"You bet. Who's on offer?" said Sam.

"To you? Just about anybody in pants, my beauty. Has my mother jumped the gun on me for Sunday dinner?"

"She has, but I didn't answer."

"What strength of character you must have," he said admiringly. "How did you get away without answering?"

"I sidetracked her."

"You sidetracked my *mother?* With what? A Sherman tank?"

They were laughing now. Funny how she'd never before realized quite how intimate shared laughter could be. "We got on to all the lonely people in the world who need to find suitable partners."

"No, that's not good enough. She came back at you."

Sam couldn't stop smiling. "You know her very well. I spoke very firmly to her. I said if you wanted to see me again you'd ask."

"Quite right. Consider yourself asked. Can you come?"

She supposed if Justin had had anything important on the cards for Sunday, like theatre tickets or anything like that, he would have mentioned it before this. "Yes, thank you."

"So now, give me the straight goods—do women like men in white cotton underwear?"

"Women like men in anything."

"Ah...how pleased I am to hear it. I'll be out of town till late Saturday. May I pick you up on Sunday evening at about six?"

"Yes," she said.

There was a curious feeling like hunger in her stomach when she hung up. She realized it was anticipation.

6

![decorative divider]

'Shall we go out and look at some places on Saturday?'' Justin asked on Tuesday night over dinner.

For some reason, she found she was staring at her plate. ''Oh! I—I guess so.'' She forced herself to look at him. What on earth was the matter with her? She smiled. ''What's the alternative?''

He shrugged. ''I've been thinking about whether to put in an offer on that penthouse at The Romanoff. What's your opinion?''

She frowned, unsure of the name. ''Was that the first one we saw?''

''Darling, you know it was. I must say, I like those buildings, The Romanoff, The Tudor, The Bourbon. They've chosen the locations very well. And they're soundly built. What do you think?''

''Justin, isn't it about five times bigger than anything you need?''

He smiled. ''You say that because you're not used to entertaining on a grand scale.''

This irritated her. It was rare for her to feel irritation with Justin. ''You don't entertain on a grand scale, Justin. In fact, you entertain less than I do. At least I cook dinner for you and Merc and Larry now and then, and have the odd party.''

"You're right." He made a face. "I've been riding on Veronica's coattails for too long. I only meant that it would take you a while to get into the swing of things, but once you did, I think you'd find you were very glad of the space."

There it was again, the half-promise and innuendo. She'd been feeding off it for weeks now, not objecting to Justin's oblique approach, but suddenly a little puff of anger ignited in the pit of her stomach, so the embers must have been there without her knowing.

He was taking a lot for granted, wasn't he? He was assuming that when—if!—he chose to firm up his offer, she would be waiting for it. He was assuming there was no danger of another man wanting her. She thought of Ben Harris saying, "anybody in pants, my beauty" and wondered why it never seemed to occur to Justin that some other man might find her as desirable as he did.

It was half her fault, of course, because she had conspired in it. She'd always smiled at his comments and left them unchallenged, as though she was perfectly happy to be left "on approval" for as long as Justin needed to make up his mind. As though she were the beggar at the gates.

Well, she could at least change that. She could withdraw her collusion.

Sam opened her eyes at him and said, "Are you hoping I'll take over your catering in place of Veronica after you've moved, Justin?"

He blinked, but recovered quickly, smiling at her in the way he had that made her stomach melt. She couldn't have said why, she was even shocked by her own thought—but suddenly she wondered if that compelling smile was ever calculated. Did Justin *know* what effect it had?

"Darling, I thought we had an understanding." He spoke reproachfully. She was aware that in ordinary circumstances she would have smiled at this and let the moment pass. She failed to ask herself why this was not "ordinary circumstances."

"Did you? What did you think I understood?"

"Darling, do you want a declaration? Is that what it is?" Justin asked, with a tender amusement that said she was foolish and sweet.

Of course it was what she wanted. To feel cherished and secure, to know that he loved her enough to want to be certain of her. And yet . . .

All at once, she was panicking. She loved him, she knew she loved him, but marriage, or living together—whatever Justin had in mind—was a big step, after all. Not so easy to change your mind after the fact if you found you'd made a mistake . . .

Maybe she should take more time. Maybe Justin had been right to be so cautious. Surely she should be absolutely certain of her own feelings, her own commitment.

"Justin—"

It was as if he sensed that sudden, inner withdrawal, recognized the threat in it. He leaned towards her over the tabletop, reached out and grasped her hand. "Sam, darling," he said, smiling at her with that melting blue gaze, "shall we get married?"

So it was marriage after all, some dry, uninvolved part of her mind noted. She hadn't wanted it to be like this, the question forced out of him, and herself unexpectedly full of doubt. That was why she wasn't as overjoyed as she'd imagined being. But it *was* what she

wanted, she knew that, even if for some perverse reason it didn't make her as overwhelmingly happy as it
should right at this moment. She desperately wanted
to feel the love and security that Justin's ring on her
finger would offer her, the sense of belonging, to know
that he loved her and she loved him. And momentary
doubt in the face of such a commitment—surely that
was to be expected?

"Darling?" he prompted.

Her heart was shaking like a sail that had lost the
wind. What on earth was wrong with her? *Say yes!*
someone inside commanded her. Sam obediently
opened her mouth, but that wasn't what came out.
"Justin, please don't ask me that question now," she
whispered instead, her head bent.

He laughed irritably. "Now, come, darling! Is this
pique? Has it been so wrong of me to imagine that we
understood each other? Should I have swept you off
your feet?" He paused. "I wish I had."

The cajolery in his voice worked on her, as always,
convincing her that she had been wrong. Had he really
believed that she had taken it for granted? Maybe it
was just pique, as he said, and not panic at all. And
yet, all this time she had been so certain that he was
still considering, still unsure....

"Look at me, Sam!"

She looked up. He was holding her hand, and smiling deep into her eyes, and the magic suddenly worked
again.

"Do you love me?" he asked softly.

"Yes," she said. Of course she loved him. She had
loved him since the day she walked into his office the
first time and the sun had been shining through a
mellow old window onto his fair head.

"Well, that solves the problem of what to do on Saturday," Justin said. "We're going to buy you a ring!" He paused thoughtfully. "And I think I will put in an offer for The Romanoff, darling. I'll go substantially lower than the asking, of course, test the water first."

Sam smiled because she must, because she knew she was happy even if she didn't feel it right now. Of course it was absolutely normal to feel just a little trapped. Newly engaged women did. Her life was going to change out of all recognition, it was natural she would be feeling panicky. But of course she was deliriously happy underneath.

Ben climbed into the driver's seat, and then, in the moment of leaning forward to start the engine, he paused. His dark gaze raked her in the evening sunshine.

"What have you been doing to yourself?" he demanded.

Sam faced him in surprise, her hand on the seatbelt lock. "Nothing in particular. Why?"

He shrugged. "I don't know. You look strained, as if you were under too much stress all of a sudden. What's the problem?"

She laughed and turned away, his scrutiny making her uncomfortable. Was that the way he looked at the people he photographed? His pictures were always so uncomfortable, as though his camera saw some inner truth. With his gaze on her, she understood that it wasn't the camera that saw through the surface of things, but Ben Harris's eyes.

But there was no reason for it to make her uncomfortable. She had nothing to hide, no inner truth that contradicted the outer. "There's no problem, Ben. Just the opposite. Justin asked me to marry him on Tuesday."

He wasn't moving anyway, but there was a new sense of stillness, alertness, about him. "Ah. And what did you answer?"

"I said yes, of course." Though in fact she hadn't, she realized with a little flick of shock. She had never actually said yes. But of course Justin had known it was what she wanted.

Ben reached out and picked up her naked left hand. His finger and thumb pressed hard where her ring should be, almost as if he were making his own mark there. A shiver went through her. She thought inconsequently that a proposal from Ben would be a very different, probably far less civilised, affair than Justin's had been. If he ever decided to settle for one woman, of course.

"Thanks for leaving off the ring tonight. I don't think the charade would be quite so effective if they saw you with another man's ring on your finger," Ben said, while at the back of his mind was the insane conviction that if she *had* been wearing the ring he would have dragged it off and tossed it out the window.

"The ring is being made specially. We chose the stones at the jeweller's yesterday," she told him. A large, very beautiful diamond and two small pale turquoises. Justin had been determined to be conventional. "Darling, of course it's got to be diamonds," he'd insisted, when the glow of a ruby had caught her eye. The one he and the jeweller had decided on in the end wasn't exactly the Kohinoor, but it was the biggest diamond Sam had ever seen close up.

"Have you told him about this game we're playing?" Ben's voice cut firmly across her thoughts, and she lifted her head and blinked her shadowed green eyes at him. She'd been staring absently at his fingers on her hand.

Her head was close to his; he could smell her perfume softly riding over the smells of autumn. He realized that he wanted to kiss her. The knowledge made him furious with her fiancé. What was he doing, letting her loose like this? The man was a fool. Any woman who was engaged to Ben wouldn't be pretending to be dating another man, no matter how innocent the game was. The thought travelled involuntarily from his brain to his fingertips, as though he were leaving his seal on her flesh.

He stared into her eyes. Man, she had some chemistry. Maybe this charade hadn't been the smartest thing he'd ever dreamt up.

He released her hand and turned to start the car. He was wrong. He had left no mark on her.

"I said I was going out to dinner with friends," Sam answered huskily, drawing back from him. Her ring finger felt oddly sensitive, a little prickly, as if Ben had left some kind of trace there. "There's no reason for him to know all about it. It's not as though it's a *real* date, after all. Anyway, Justin never pries. He trusts me."

She wasn't sure why she was being so defensive. Something in his eyes had challenged her, and she knew she was overexplaining.

Ben braked at a stop sign and used the moment to glance at her. "And does he trust me?" *Or any man,* he was thinking. Was the man blind as well as a fool?

She had forgotten how easily he could put her stomach into free fall. "He doesn't know anything about you, so there's no reason for him to trust or distrust you."

"If he doesn't know about me specifically, he must know there are men around you."

"Well, what do you expect him to do?" she demanded irritably. "He's proposed, and I've accepted. The ring is being made. What would *you* do? Put me in a pumpkin shell?"

The dark eyes were sweeping over her again, in a quick, curiously possessive gaze, as though even imagining himself her fiancé was enough to make him jealous.

He said, knowing it was true, "If you had accepted my proposal and the ring couldn't be ready immediately, you'd be wearing something on that finger, even if it were only a twisted paper clip."

Sam absently rubbed the base of her ring finger, where he had touched her. She thought, half unconsciously, I *am* wearing something. I'm wearing your touch, and I'll never be free of it. But it was a crazy thought, and she shook it off. "I told you, he trusts me."

He flicked her a glance, though traffic was heavy.

"He's a fool, then."

She gasped with astonishment and rage.

Before she could speak, he said, "You don't love him enough to marry him. God knows why you've convinced yourself you do, but the man's got his work cut out for him, making this stick. He'd better recognize that fact and get down to it before you come to your senses. And the first thing he should be doing is keeping other men away."

She was swept with sudden, total fury. "How *dare* you?" she demanded. "Of course I love him! What do you know about it, anyway?" She wanted to hit him right across his smug face.

"I know you're looking a helluva lot more stressed today than you did Monday," Ben said flatly, irritated by her stubborn blindness. Of course she didn't love the guy, not that it was any of his business. Not that he cared if she made a mess of things. "That says something, doesn't it?"

"It says nothing! That has nothing whatever to do with Justin! I've been working hard! I was up most of Monday night, and I haven't caught up on my sleep yet, that's all!"

"Bull," Ben said, screeching to an unnecessarily hard stop at a yellow light. "You've just made a major life-changing decision, and that's far more important than anything in the daily grind. I've seen people who were under daily bombardment, starving and freezing and drinking putrid water, make the decision to get married. They light up like bulbs, in spite of the hell around them." He looked over at her again as he turned a corner. "If they've made the right choice."

He didn't say, "which you have not," but the words were there in the air.

He was pushing her further into certainty. Of course she loved Justin. She was thrilled, absolutely thrilled, at the thought of becoming his wife.

"Maybe I reserve my bulb-lighting for Justin's eyes," she said coldly.

Ben was flooded with an anger that he didn't recognize. Irritation with her stupidity, maybe, because she was walking into the biggest mistake you could make in life.

"Don't be stupid," he said harshly.

"What the hell do you know about it?" Sam demanded furiously, losing her grip on her temper. "You're an expert on the subject of love, are you?"

"It doesn't take an expert. Anybody could tell you. You look like Death on a bicycle."

But she was still talking. "You, the man who's had more women than he's had hot dinners? And I do *not* look like Death on a bicycle!" she added, belatedly hearing his last comment. It only drove her further into fury that Marie had said much the same thing. *What's worrying you about it? Aren't you happy?* Marie had said. "I've been working hard and haven't had enough sleep this week!"

"More women that I've— Who the hell told you that?" Ben shouted over her last sentence. What the hell was she talking about? A horn challenged him from behind, and he realized the light he didn't remember stopping at was green. He couldn't be sure it had been red when he braked. He put his foot on the gas, and the other car swerved out to pass and laid rubber halfway up the street.

"Who needs to be told? It's at least as obvious as the 'fact' that I don't love Justin!"

"*I* need to be told! I have not had more women than hot dinners, and I'd like to know where you think you got that idea! And I didn't say you didn't love him! I said you didn't love him enough to marry him!"

They were shouting at each other like—he didn't know like what. This was ridiculous. Ben couldn't figure out what the hell was making him so mad. It was her life, after all, and what did he care what she imagined about his sex life?

"And I've told you I do! And you said yourself that your mother has thrown a bottomless supply of chesty blondes at you, and the ones you bring home yourself never last the course! To a simple soul like me that seems to add up."

"Would you do me the simple honour," Ben began, with furious restraint, "not to imagine that I screw everybody who is thrown at my head?"

"Maybe if you stopped telling me Justin was a fool to trust you with me I wouldn't imagine it!" Sam countered. "Will you do *me* the simple honour not to imagine that I don't know my own feelings?"

The car drew up outside the Harrises' house, under a brilliant orange tree that hadn't yet lost its leaves. A bright leaf fluttered down onto the windshield, followed by another, as though in greeting. But Ben and Sam both were beyond being charmed by the sight. Sam flung open her door, and then, caught by her seatbelt, turned back to undo it.

"I don't say you don't know your own feelings," Ben said, with a quiet, deadly meaning that simply took her breath away. She stared at him, her face white with fury, her green eyes almost black.

"How *dare* you?" she screeched. "What are you saying? That I'm marrying him for his money? Is that what you're saying?"

"I don't know," Ben said levelly, staring right into her impassioned gaze. He raised his eyebrows. "Is he rich?"

"Oh! You really are—" She bit off the epithet, got out, slammed the door, stormed up the walk and dashed up the verandah steps. Determined to get away from him before she was reduced to hitting the arrogant bastard, she rang the doorbell with exactly the kind of urgency that always irritated her, and heard it pealing through the house. Behind her the car engine died, and the car door slammed. In front of her, the house door opened.

"Sam! Hi! Come on in," said Miranda, with a broad smile. "I thought Ben was picking you up. Is he going to be late?"

"He'll be late enough if I get my hands on him!" Sam announced, through her teeth. "He'll be the late, great Ben Harris!"

He came lightly up the steps behind her, and she felt the vibration in every vertebra. "Hi, Mom," he said.

Miranda looked from one to the other. Sam's face was flushed, her eyes gleaming with anger, her chest heaving. Ben's own eyes were glittering in a way his mother knew well. He didn't lose his temper often, but when he did, he did it in spades.

"Are you two fighting?" Miranda demanded, stepping back to let them in.

"No," they both said simultaneously, in furious tones that made the lie so obvious Miranda went off into a peal of laughter.

"What on earth can you have found to fight about on your second meeting?" she marvelled.

"Just the regular," Sam answered stupidly, for something to say.

Miranda screeched with laughter. "The *regular?* The regular *what?*"

Her throaty, infectious laughter was having an effect. Of course it was ridiculous. What on earth *had* they been fighting about? The whole thing was simply made up out of whole cloth. Sam began to smile involuntarily, her rage transmogrifying with surprising suddenness into a bubble of laughter. Her eyes involuntarily found Ben's.

"Oh, you know, Mom," he said, shrugging. He was laughing himself now, right into Sam's eyes, his rage dissolving. He discovered a renewed—or continuing, he couldn't be sure—desire to kiss her. In fact, he wanted to do more than kiss her. "Whether to send the kids to private school."

"All right, don't tell me," his mother said. She took Sam's coat and led her into the sitting room, laughing so hard she was wiping her eyes by this time.

Ben followed more slowly, thinking. He wasn't sure what had made him explode like that. So she was making a mistake, so what? It wasn't his business, he reminded himself. There was no reason to take anything personally here. Anyway, maybe what she said was true. Maybe she was saving the light bulb for the cold-blooded specimen she was going to marry. Why was he so sure he was right?

It occurred to him briefly that he would like to see Sam with her inner light turned on—it would be some sight, all right. He would even like to be the one who supplied the electricity. But the thought disappeared as soon as it formed.

7

It was a smaller group that sat down to dinner that night. Matt and Ella and Luke and Carol were there, but Simon and Alice had spent the weekend at the family summer cottage and were probably caught in traffic, or had decided not to come down till Monday morning. The only new face was Sara, Jude's girlfriend, a tall, incredibly slim black girl who looked like a model to Sam, but who was planning to study veterinary medicine.

Judith was there. She didn't seem at all in predatory mode, but Sam wondered whether Ella was still hoping her friend would be able to carry off her brother. Not that it mattered to her, but she had to remind herself that it might still be considered her duty to deflect Ben's attention that way.

In spite of the reduction in actual numbers, the noise level didn't seem to be any lower than it had been last week. It wasn't that everyone always talked at once, though it sometimes felt that way to Sam, who wasn't used to such rowdiness. It was that everyone always responded to whatever was said. The conversation was punctuated with laughs, groans, agreement or good-natured vilification and extremely quick repartee. It was like being at a three-ring circus, not that Sam had ever had that pleasure.

They had coffee and liqueurs in the sitting room after the meal. Sam, in black leggings and a loose sweater, sat on the floor beside Miranda's chair, chatting quietly to her about little in particular while a much louder conversation went on on the other side of the room among the men.

The contrast between Ben's looks and those of his brothers and father was very strong, Sam thought absently, not just in physique and colouring but in their *being*. The blond giants all sat four-square, leaning forward with their elbows on their knees, sometimes leaning back with an ankle crossed over a knee. Their gestures tended to be broad, their laughter and voices loud. Natural extroverts, every one.

Ben, on the other hand, often had a lazy posture, spoke softly, and his gestures were much less expansive. None of this lessened his impact. When any of the blond giants spoke, the others might easily talk right over him, but when Ben spoke, she noticed they were mostly quiet, listening.

And it wasn't that he was always imparting specialised information, either. They all clearly knew much more than Ben did about cars, for example, and yet when he made a comment even about that subject, they listened. As though they were in the habit, somehow, or as though something about him just commanded their unconscious respect.

Sam turned to look up at Miranda, not having heard the last few sentences, and, in an absent way speaking her thoughts aloud, answered whatever the last question had been with, "But he doesn't look like you, either." Miranda was slim for her size, but she was a big-boned woman with small facial features quite unlike Ben's.

Miranda smiled at her, following her thoughts through the medium of having followed her gaze. She had watched Ben watching Sam, too, their gazes always just missing each other. Their radar was good. Neither looked up when the other was watching, or when the one looked up, the other's eyes slid away. They took it in turns.

Of course she should have realized that in the end Ben would fall for someone completely against his own type. Such a stubborn man as he was, he would have to thwart even his own tastes. And of course Justin McCourt wasn't the man for Sam. No man could be who had Veronica Taggart for a mother and Hal McCourt for a father. Formaldehyde where their blood should be. Sam had lots of good red blood in her veins. Just like Ben. Whatever excuse Sam was giving herself that allowed her to date Ben, Miranda knew that in reality she was dating him because, though she might not know it yet, he was right for her and Justin wasn't. And she wasn't married to Justin yet.

"Arthur isn't Ben's natural father," Miranda said calmly, keeping her thoughts to herself. "I had Ben when I was seventeen. When Arthur married me he adopted Ben. He promised to raise him as his own, and he never went back on that."

"Oh!" Sam glanced back at the men with this new knowledge, not noticing, as Miranda did, Ben's gaze shift from her face. Yes, of course. She might have guessed it, really. "He's very different, isn't he? You were right about that."

With satisfaction, Miranda noted that use of the word "he". As though there were only one man in the room.

"His father was the same. A very electric, vital, creative man. Like a power force. I was done for before he even said hello."

"How did you meet him?" Sam asked with real interest.

Miranda smiled with the memory. "Well, I was an early hippie. Before that name was even coined. 'Beatnik' was the word then. I used to hang out down in the Village—Yorkville Avenue, you know. It was full of coffee shops and men playing chess and guitars.

"Michael was playing a guitar in some dark basement, singing folk songs. I came in one night when he was singing, 'Kumbaya'."

Sam saw that Miranda's eyes were distant now, and the smile on her lips somehow made her look young.

"He was sitting there with the light from a candle flickering behind him, and I stopped at the door—a tiny basement room with a few chairs and tables—and just stared at him. He was like a dark angel. He didn't seem like any man I'd ever met. He saw me staring at him, and then he sang 'Someone's smilin', Lord, Kumbaya', the whole verse, to me . . . his eyes told me he was the someone smiling, because he was looking at me. . . . Well."

She glanced at Ben and then down at Sam, coming out of her trance. "Every girl should lose her virginity in such a passionate way. He treated me badly afterwards, I suppose, but I have never regretted those few months. Anyway, it wasn't really his fault—I was young and had no idea how to handle him. When I look back now, I see that if I'd been a bit smarter, more mature, he'd have ended up marrying me. Of course, I'm glad he didn't, now. It wouldn't have worked, with Ben coming. Arthur's been a far better father to Ben than Michael would ever have been.''

Sam was fascinated by the story, and wanted to keep her talking. ''Really? Better than his own father?''

''Oh, Michael was far too artistic, too intense. He's still married to Patricia, God knows how she can stand it, but she certainly never made the mistake of having children. Ben had what a boy of his temperament needed—a stable masculine influence to ground all that intensity and sparky intelligence. Ben has good, solid values. You'll see. You'll never have to worry about *him* leaving you in the lurch.''

That brought Sam back to earth with a bang. She sat up and fixed Miranda with a look. ''Andy—you promised!'' she said firmly.

Miranda clapped a remorseful hand to her mouth. ''Oh, Sam! I'm sorry, I forgot! It's just second nature with me, I'm afraid!'' She burst out laughing, looking at Sam from eyes brimming over with humour and approval. Sam couldn't resist the invitation, and laughed herself. Miranda shook her head. She would have to get a guard on her tongue if she was going to get these two... ''I didn't mean anything by it. I know you're very happy.''

''Very happy,'' Sam agreed. Suddenly she wished Justin had bought her a ready-made ring. She had nothing to hold on to, nothing to remind her of reality. If she let down her guard, she might be swept away in a storm.

* * *

"You and Mom were enjoying each other," Ben observed on the way home.

"She was telling me what a good provider you'd be."

"Were you itching to tell her what a good one you've already got? My provisions don't come anywhere near McCourt standards."

"I don't look on Justin as a provider, thank you."

"Good thing," he remarked cryptically. "What else were you two talking about? She wasn't outlining my sins, I'm sure. Too smart to be talking down the merchandise."

"You're sure we were talking about you, are you?" Sam said with a smile.

"With Miranda, it seems a safe bet."

He turned a corner into a quiet, tree-lined street, and light from a street lamp flashed across her eyes in the darkness.

Suddenly, with a loud chirping of rubber against asphalt, he slammed on the brakes. Three figures running pell mell from a house tore onto the road immediately in front of the car, leapt awkwardly around the front bumper, and dashed across to the other side of the street.

Sam gasped and involuntarily flung her hands up, her adrenalin pumping the ready response to danger into her bloodstream even though no action was possible.

"How did you *see* them so fast?" she demanded breathlessly. It was amazing no one had been hit.

Ben kept his foot on the brake and glanced towards the house the men had come from. Sam followed his gaze and only now saw the broken window, the door left swinging open.

"Phone in the glove compartment," he said calmly. "I guess you'd better call the cops."

He let up on the brake and drove on.

Sam picked up the phone and dialled the police emergency number. She looked over at him as she waited for the police to answer. "All in a day's work?" she asked. She supposed being in the midst of war so often sharpened the senses.

Ben shrugged. "Up to a point. The streetlight threw a long shadow."

She reported the incident to the policewoman who answered the call, and was immediately transferred to a police frequency, repeating all the details to a couple of patrol cars in the area.

A few minutes later they were at her front door. Sam was regretting that that earlier conversation had been cut off. She was curious to know what Ben thought Andy would have been telling her about him. "Would you like to come up?" she suggested.

He turned and looked at her, and Sam swallowed. "I mean . . . maybe you need to calm down a little?"

He grinned, his teeth flashing in the night, and she smiled sheepishly. Anybody who looked less as if they needed calming down would be hard to find. "I guess not," she amended, before he could speak.

"Do you want me to see you inside?" he asked. "Are you nervous?" She wasn't. Before she had even known there was danger, Ben had been coping with it. Her heart wasn't even thumping.

"No, I just thought—"

He reached out and brushed her cheek with an electric touch. "You thought I needed to calm down."

He supplied the words softly. "But it wouldn't calm me down to go upstairs with you at this hour of the night, Sam. So I'd better say no, don't you think?"

Her heart was thumping now, all right. It was in her ears, deafening her. "Yes...ah, yeah, well, good night, then." Sam was stammering like a sixteen-year-old.

"On the other hand, Miranda will certainly ask what we did tonight," he said, his hand drifting down to cup her chin. She felt the firm strength of the thin fingers and remembered how he had kissed her last Monday. *One way to be sure we get our stories straight,* he'd said then.

Sam gasped as she made the connection, and he felt the pulse jump in her throat under his touch. His own heart rate shifted in response, and he slowly leaned towards her.

Behind them, bright headlights turned the corner, and a car pulled up beside them, its engine purring. A window rolled down, and Ben sat up and pressed the control to put his own window down.

"Evening, Officer," he said.

"Good evening, sir. Did you report the house-breaking over on Branach Street?" They had asked for her name and address when she called in, so it was a pretty safe guess.

"Yeah, we did. Did you manage to get them?"

"A patrol car saw them, but they fled on foot into a backyard. We've got a couple of cars out cruising the streets in the area now, hoping to pick them up. Anything you can add to the description of any of them?"

Ben described the men he'd seen in the road, and Sam added what she could, and then the policeman said good-night, and moved quietly away again.

For Sam, the interruption had restored her to common sense and sanity. Last week, when Ben had kissed her, she had been technically still free. Tonight, ring or no ring, she was an engaged woman. "Good night, Ben," she said.

He pulled the key out of the ignition. "I'll see you to the door," he said, so matter-of-factly that she knew he was thinking about the three men, and not about making a move on her.

She was right. Inside the door he merely bent his head to touch her cheek lightly with his lips. "Good night. Sleep well," he said, and she watched him moving with well-knitted ease down the walk to his car, with a feeling that might or might not have been regret.

Justin didn't like the set of the turquoises. Rather than a more conventional arrangement with the diamond in between the two, he had chosen one where both turquoises sat high on one side of the diamond, at about ten o'clock.

But he didn't quite like the way the design had been executed. "The turquoises are set too close together," he said to the jeweller. "I wanted a little breathing room between them."

His words took on a curious weight, in the way a simple statement sometimes does, and Sam glanced up at him. "Is that symbolic, Justin?" she asked with a smile.

"Darling, I'd be the last man on earth to quote cheap philosophy in a ring." He turned back to the jeweller. "Do you see what I mean? This one just a little higher, that's all it needs."

The jeweller was making notes on the brown envelope, and Sam realized that she wasn't going to get her ring today. Her chest constricted, and she laid her hand over Justin's, where he held the ring between thumb and forefinger.

"Darling, it's very beautiful," she said softly. "Couldn't we just take it as it is?" *If you'd accepted my proposal and the ring couldn't be ready immediately, you'd be wearing something on that finger, even if it were only a twisted paper clip,* she heard, and abruptly she wanted to know that Justin really wanted her, cherished her, that it was with him she belonged.

"Now, darling, don't panic, I'm not going to change my mind, you know, just because the ring's another week coming," Justin said comfortably.

Hearing those words, she went momentarily still, a fact that Justin did not notice but the jeweller did. "Oh, what a relief," she replied tonelessly.

The jeweller, a large, jowly Asian in late middle-age, raised an eyebrow at her and made a face that told her *he* at least thought Justin had his priorities wrong, and that, as she was still free, she might just use the opportunity to think again. Sam bit her lip and dropped her head, trying not to laugh.

Justin was oblivious to all this, a fact that surprised her. She'd always thought him so sensitive, so quick to pick up on nuance. But he was going away tomorrow, and of course he was preoccupied with getting a million things done today. Concentration on something else did interfere with one's sensitivity.

"Do you mind if I leave you to make your own way home, Sam?" Justin asked as they came out into the bright fall sunshine. "I've got to drop in at Gucci and get a new strap for my bag, and then I've got a dozen other errands, and I can do it all faster on my own. You know the shops will be a madhouse today.''

"Yeah, okay, Justin," she said. She reached up to kiss his cheek lightly. "Have a good trip."

It was perhaps a little too easy, her agreement. Perhaps he had expected her to insist on coming, to promise to stick to his coattails as he dashed in and out of the stores. Or perhaps her sudden coolness transmitted itself on some level. "Wait a minute, that's no goodbye," Justin said. His arms came up around her, and his mouth found hers with firm possession.

They were a very chic couple, Justin so tall, slim and blond, in the right loafers and the right tweedy jacket; Sam slender and pale, with her black hair in a neat chignon and wearing the smartly tailored jacket and pants Justin had chosen for her. Not quite the people you ordinarily saw kissing passionately in the middle of Yonge Street on a Saturday morning. People smiled as they skirted them, but two people stopped for a moment, watching.

"Sam!" one of them trilled, when Justin lifted his lips again. Sam looked around.

"Oh, hi, Ella! Hi, Judith!" It occurred to her that Judith was looking at her with cool reproach. "Come and meet Justin! Justin . . . Ella, Judith."

He would never see them again, so there wasn't much point going into potted bios, Sam told herself, not quite understanding why she was reluctant to do so.

"I've seen you around campus, haven't I? Aren't you Justin McCourt? Department of English?" said Ella, shaking his hand.

In another minute, Justin had said goodbye and gone striding down the street, his pale hair glinting in the sun. "Shall we go for a coffee?" Ella demanded.

Judith didn't have time before a hair appointment, so they walked her down the street to the salon and left her. She was still looking frosty, and scarcely glanced at Sam when they said goodbye.

"Why is Judith angry with me?" Sam demanded, as soon as she was seated across from Ella in a coffee shop. "If looks could kill!"

Ella laughed. "Well, you see, that was a pretty thorough kiss he was giving you, Sam, right there in the middle of the street."

Sam supposed it was, but she had been feeling piqued with him, and it hadn't had the usual impact of Justin's kisses on her. "And that bothered Judith? Why?"

"Well, honey, you see—Judith thinks Ben is your fiancé," Ella said. Sam gasped. "Don't you remember?"

"But—but everybody just laughed! Didn't anybody tell her that was a joke?" She had thought the family's reaction had made it obvious the whole thing was a joke.

Ella had a beautiful, slow smile, her wide, full lips flattening and then parting over fabulous white teeth, her eyes glinting as she shared life's marvellous humour with you. Sam felt the laughter rising, just watching that smile.

"No, why should we?"

"Well—don't you want—I mean, I thought you wanted Ben to get interested in Judith."

"Well, I did, but he didn't."

"He might, though."

Sipping her coffee, Ella shook her head. "Hmm. Ben's never lukewarm, and anyway, Judith's not the kind of woman who has to grow on a man, is she? Instant impact, that's what she is."

"So she thinks I'm cheating on Ben with Justin?" Sam rolled her eyes.

"And what are you really doing?" Ella asked. "Having second thoughts?"

"What?"

"Andy says you're engaged to Justin."

"I am. That jeweller's you saw us coming out of is making my ring."

"I guess I'm stupid. What are you doing with Ben, then? Andy reckons you don't know your own mind."

It was as though a chasm opened at her feet. What on earth kind of tangle was she getting herself into, making half the world imagine she was cheating on Justin with Ben, and the other half that she was cheating on Ben with Justin?

"It's not my business," Ella said, seeing Sam's face.

"Oh, boy," said Sam, staring unseeingly down into her coffee. "Oh, I should never have let her talk me into starting this! What a mess! What if Justin found out? He'd never believe the truth!"

"Would Ben?" Ella asked gently, and of course it was Ben who was her concern. She didn't care about Justin—or Sam, come to that.

"Ben *knows!*" Sam said desperately. "It's Ben I'm doing it for!" She looked up. "You see, Ella, I'm helping Andy run a scam on Ben, all right, but I'm also helping Ben run a scam on Andy. Please don't tell her."

"*What?*"

"Yeah, I'm supposed to be the decoy, but suddenly I feel one heck of a lot more like a sitting duck!"

8

➤◄

'Sam? It's Merc.''

"Hi, Mercedes. Everything all right?"

"Well, no. Larry's had a horrible cold since Tues-day, and it's turning into flu. I've managed to con-vince him to stay in bed this morning, and, Sam, I don't think you should come around tonight. He's not going to be able to go to work tomorrow, and I don't think this is something you want to catch."

Sam almost protested. She almost said she would rather catch the flu than be alone tonight of all nights. But of course she didn't. She had lots of good friends, but there was no one to whom she could say, "This is November fourth and I'd rather not be alone."

Of course she would be fine. She was missing Jus-tin, that was the problem. The first week of his ab-sence had moved slowly. He had been in Venice that week, at a three-day academic conference where he had delivered a paper. Next week there was another conference in Germany.

Naturally Sam would have liked to go with him, but at first it was only going to be three days in Venice, and Justin was going to be in the conference most of the time. Venice was too romantic a city to see on your own. The invitation to the Berlin conference had come later, when her work schedule was already full. She had four deadlines over the two weeks.

Now she was wishing she had taken a lap-top and gone. There had been a nip in the air all day, and she hated the onset of winter.

"Tell Larry I hope he's feeling better soon," she said instead. She hung up, and then, with a yearning that surprised her, she was thinking of dinner at the Harrises. Of course she couldn't go. She'd made up her mind, and she wasn't going again. That meeting with Judith and Ella had showed her how foolish she had been to imagine she could play such a game without getting entangled in misunderstandings. She was putting an end to the masquerade, though she hadn't told Ben or Miranda yet.

It was two weeks since she'd seen them. Once she'd legitimately been to dinner at the McCourts, but last Sunday she'd simply said she had too much to do. And it was true she had a lot of work piled up.

But somehow she hadn't been able to concentrate. Eight o'clock that night had found her knocking on Marie's door, with a big bowl of unbuttered popcorn, but the model had had a five o'clock call Monday morning and had thrown her out at nine, right in the middle of *Casablanca*. "Rent the video," she'd said heartlessly, when Sam protested. "It's being messed up with commercial breaks anyway. And you've seen it a zillion times. It's not as if you don't know how it ends."

"You'll regret this, sweetheart," Sam warned her darkly. "Maybe not now, maybe not tomorrow, but soon, and for the rest of your life." Then she'd gone to bed early, with a book. Fortunately page fifty-eight was riveting, because she read it about a dozen times before giving up.

And here it was Sunday again. It was cold, winter was coming and she had nothing in the place for dinner except a packet of macaroni and cheese, which was long past its "Eat By" date.

The phone rang, and she knew before she picked it up who it was.

"It's Andy," said Miranda. "Are you coming for dinner tonight, Sam? Ben says he's not sure."

She sounded so casually friendly, as if Sam had been going there on Sunday for years. Sam looked out the window and saw the first three snowflakes of the season whisper against the glass and then scurry away.

"Oh—no, I'm—" She paused, swallowing. If only Andy had called before Merc, if only she had a cast-iron excuse. If only it weren't snowing. If only it weren't November 4. "No," Sam said, more gruffly than she intended. "I told Ben, but I guess he forgot. Thanks anyway, but I can't."

Miranda could feel it all slipping away. Damn Judith, anyway. Why had she been on that piece of pavement for that critical minute, and where did she get her uptight morals from, anyway, with parents like hers? Reaction, Andy supposed. If only Niki had been a little *more* conventional, no doubt her daughter would be a little *less*. Last time Andy had been in Vancouver, Niki had still been wearing the long flowing print dresses and long flowing hair they'd both worn in the sixties.

"You look like an aging hippie, Niki," Andy had warned her friend, and Niki had answered, unarguably, "Andy, this is *Vancouver*."

"Ella told me what happened," Andy said now. "I just want to say that Judith isn't coming tonight, Sam."

"It isn't just that, Andy."

"What is it, then?"

"Oh, I—" Sam felt so *tired* suddenly, as though everything was too much for her. How could she explain the dangerous seductiveness of the Harrises, or the way she had so dispassionately watched the Mc-Courts two Sundays ago and realized for the first time that their coldness of demeanour might signal an actual coldness of heart? Up till now she had always assumed that it was just their way—they didn't hug, they didn't kiss, they didn't laugh much, but they loved each other underneath, she'd always thought. Now, for the first time, she was wondering.

And she didn't want to be dispassionately wondering about her future in-laws in this way. She didn't want to be always comparing them, consciously or unconsciously, to the Harrises.

Of course, Justin was truly warm-hearted and sensitive under the McCourt exterior, but when he was with his family she didn't like him nearly as well as when she had him on his own. Still, the less she saw of the Harrises, the better.

"Are you doing something else tonight?"

"Well..."

"Everybody wants to see you. We've missed you. Please come."

The three snowflakes had come back, bringing a hundred friends. They were throwing themselves menacingly at the glass, as if they wanted to come in and freeze her.

"Oh, Miranda—I just—"

"Great. I'll tell Ben to pick you up as usual, at six," Miranda said. "Dress up warm. The weatherman says winter's coming."

"Snow mellows the Harrises, I see," Sam commented that night, as Ben slowly drove her home through streets made perilous by the thick, sudden blanket that had descended all day and was still coming down.

"Lots of things mellow the Harrises. But never for very long at a time." It had been a subdued, gentle evening tonight, the Harrises sitting around a crackling wood fire discussing Christmas plans and the imminent birth of Carol's baby with smiles in their voices. "Did you enjoy it, nonetheless?"

The car skidded very gently at a red light. Ben was taking the long way around, by the partly ploughed main streets. The skid made Sam suck in a little air and bite her lip. She didn't notice it herself, didn't notice Ben glancing across at her.

"What's the matter, Sam?" he asked softly.

Here on College Street the bright lights illuminated his face. "Matter?"

"You're nervous tonight. Is my family getting to you?"

"Oh...no! I like your family. It's not that I don't...no, it's something else entirely, Ben. Nothing to do with here and now at all."

He turned into a side street and there was a parking space right in front of him. He pulled over.

"Like to tell me about it?" He undid his seatbelt and turned to face her.

She shrugged, feeling foolish. "It's nothing, really. Nothing to talk about. It shouldn't still get to me, after all this time. It's just—it's the anniversary of my parents' death.''

"I'm sorry." His hand reached out and clasped hers. He drew it between both of his, and up to his mouth. Gently he kissed her fingers.

She shook her head impatiently, feeling the sympathy wrench at her heart, and suddenly she found she was talking about it. "It's a long time ago, seventeen years. It doesn't usually get to me so strongly. But—that day was the first day of winter, too. We'd had a marvellous autumn, Indian summer all though October. That afternoon, after they left, the snow started, very, very thick, and a couple of hours later it was on the news. I've always associated that smell—the smell of the first snow of the year—with that day. This year it just happens that the two coincide. The anniversary and the first snow. That's why I'm feeling it."

He didn't let go of her hand. "How did they die?"

"A plane crash. They were flying to the States. The plane crashed on landing. Something to do with the snow, I never knew exactly." She smiled mistily at him. "I've never told anyone about it in much detail before, I don't know why." It was a long time since she'd cried, too. Mourning hadn't been encouraged by the grandparents who had taken them in. It was more sensible to get on with life, and that was what Sam and Ezra had learned to do. "My mother was pregnant again, she thought it was a girl. Sometimes I can't help thinking—I'd have a sister, she'd have been seventeen next month. Sometimes I miss her as much as I do my parents."

Tears burned her eyelids, and she breathed deeply and resisted. He stroked her hair with one hand for a moment, and then, as she sighed and sat up, released her hand and turned to fasten his seatbelt and put the car in gear. Then, to her surprise, he made a U-turn.

"What are you doing? What's the matter?" Sam asked.

"Nothing. But you're not spending tonight alone. I've got a spare bed in my studio."

She would have laughed, except that it might have turned into sobs. "Ben, it's— I'll be fine."

"Yeah, I know. But you'll be a lot finer if you just relax and let me take care of things."

If her memories didn't make her cry, this kind of caring certainly would. She closed her eyes and bit her lip against the seductive certainty that Ben would not disapprove of tears.

He had the two upper floors of a beautiful old red-brick house in a pleasant residential neighbourhood not far, Sam realized, from The Romanoff. Snow coated the branches of a large oak in front and a spruce tree at the side of the house.

A private entrance at the side led up to a tiny hall-way where Ben took her coat, shucked his own and led her into a very large, comfortably proportioned living/dining room that had windows on three aspects and was filled with books. She sat down on a large sofa under the window while Ben went into the kitchen. She heard him fill a kettle with water.

He returned to the sitting room. "It's not really necessary, you know," she said again, aware that she was very grateful to be here.

"Ah, well," he said. "Humour me."

He knelt and lit a fire in the grate. It must have had a terrific draw, because the fire caught immediately and set up a friendly roar and crackle. In a few minutes he had poured brandy and brought in a tray of coffee and sliced spice cake, and then he settled down across from her.

They chatted about all kinds of things, not just her family and the dreadful change that her parents' death had forced on their lives. Ben talked about his childhood, too, and how, when Arthur Harris had said to him, "I'm your dad," he had believed him, and had never even thought of asking any questions till he was fifteen and certain things had started to add up. How he considered Arthur his "real" father, but admired his biological father as an artist.

"I didn't know he was an artist. I guess I thought he was a singer. Would I know his name?"

Ben shrugged. "I don't know. He's Michael Welsh."

Sam blinked. "Oh!" Well, that was a name important enough even for her to recognize. He was a sculptor and a painter both, and in fact—Sam began to giggle.

"What is it?" Ben asked, willing to laugh with her.

"Do you know a piece your father did titled 'Hunger'? It's kind of all thin arms and legs and children's mouths?"

Ben put down his cup and rubbed his eyes, thinking. "Oh, yeah. He did the original for I forget which building in Montreal. He did a limited edition of two or three of a smaller cast in bronze, I think."

"Well, Justin's got that in his living room."

Ben frowned in astonishment. "In his *living room?*"

"Yup."

"He lives around that thing? I mean, it's a fine piece, but he *lives* with it?" In fact, it was a great piece, but if there was one you needed distance on, 'Hunger' was it.

Sam had always felt it belonged somewhere other than the geometrical centre of that pale blond oak floor of Justin's minimalist sitting room. She liked having her opinion ratified by a real expert. She laughed again.

"Well, let's say he gets full marks for trying."

"Sam," he said, mock seriously, "you're gonna marry a living room with 'Hunger' in it?"

She couldn't help laughing. "No, no! Veronica—that's his mother, Veronica Taggart—interior designed the apartment as a showpiece. He's getting a new place. Do you know the Romanoff?"

"It's a few streets up from here, isn't it?"

"Yup. He put in an offer on the penthouse there."

For totally ostentatious wealth you could hardly go better than the Romanoff, Ben thought. He began to wonder how much that childhood trauma had made her hungry for financial security. Well, she'd certainly found it.

He sipped his brandy. "And will Veronica decorate that?"

"No. Oh, no." She nearly said, *over my dead body.* "No, Justin's prom...ah, Justin doesn't want her to. He doesn't actually like living in the showpiece, and I'm afraid he doesn't like your father's sculpture very much, except that it gets a lot of comment from visitors."

Ben bit his lip at Michael's probable comment on that. He would have to remember to tell him next time they met. Then Michael could add the McCourts to his list of "known Philistines', if they weren't already there.

* * *

It was after two before they looked at their watches, and when Sam jumped and said she had to start bright and early in the morning, he led her to his own bedroom.

"I'll sleep in the studio," he said. "If you can stand sleeping between sheets I've already slept in once, we won't bother to change them. Mrs. Martin comes on Fridays, but I was out of town till yesterday. Or would you rather have fresh ones?"

It was all so intimate, as though they'd been friends for years. She shook her head. "That's all right. Would you happen to have a guest toothbrush?"

He gave her a brand-new toothbrush, from a supply of half a dozen in the cupboard, which made her wonder, not that it was any of her business, how many of Miranda's chesty blondes he'd brought home. He also gave her a very large T-shirt. In five minutes, Sam was in his big, comfortable bed, curled up under a fluffy duvet, so cosy she'd forgotten the reason she was here.

She hadn't drawn the drapes, and she lay in bed gazing out the window after putting out the lamp, feeling warm and protected. The snow had stopped, and the night was clear. Stars twinkled, and there was moonglow on a snow-encrusted tree beside the window. The bedroom was at the top of the house, with cosily sloping ceilings, and old-fashioned eaves protected the window. The room was not unfamiliar to her. It was as though she'd slept there a hundred times, and knew all its ways, its little creaks and murmurs soothing her.

In five minutes more, she was asleep.

* * *

"Good morning."

Sam stretched and yawned, her body full of well-being. Sunlight sparkled off snow and poured into the room. She rolled over to find Ben in the doorway, wearing a loose floppy bathrobe in faded navy. Underneath, a pair of pyjamas folded generously around his ankles and bare feet.

"Good morning."

He smiled a curious smile that she couldn't read. "Did you sleep?"

"Like a dead woman."

"You're looking remarkably alive at the moment." Her eyes were bright and her cheeks and mouth a healthy pink, and it would be a good idea, Ben told himself, if he stopped enumerating her charms.

Sam giggled, sitting up and pushing her hair out of her face. No trace of morning grogginess dampened her spirits or her brain processes. "It must be the air in here," she said.

"Not the company, huh?"

"What company? I was alone all night." She pointed out severely, "You don't even have a teddy bear."

"Of course I do. Naturally he slept with me," Ben said with wounded dignity.

She hooted with laughter. "You slept with a teddy bear? I don't believe it!"

He came into the room, crossed to the closet, where he opened the door and dragged out another bathrobe, this one brand-new. He laid it on the bed. "Come with me," he said.

The room next door to the bedroom had a bare wooden floor, a desk, two chromium-and-white trestle tables and photographic equipment everywhere. In one corner was a narrow bed with a rumpled sleeping bag on it. The walls and sloping ceilings were covered with framed photographs in all sizes.

Just opposite the bed was a large picture Sam recognized. It was a city street, a bombed-out city street, filled with rubble, a derelict church tower in the distance. In the foreground a teddy bear lay abandoned. The photograph was sharp enough to show that one glass eye was missing and had been replaced with a button, and the fur on one ear was worn thin, as if from the constant stroking of a tiny, loving hand. Its paws seemed to reach out to the viewer, asking for its empty arms to be filled.

She had seen it first on the front page of a national daily, maybe two years ago.

"Was that Sarajevo?" she asked.

"Chechnya," Ben said briefly.

"It made me cry, the first time I saw that." It was a profound statement against war. She felt it pull at her again. "It's so..." But there was no word to describe the photograph's effect on the feelings.

"Oh, damn." Ben put his hand on her arm and bundled her out of the room. "I didn't mean to depress you first thing in the morning," he said, firmly closing the door.

"Can't I see the rest?" she protested.

"Not before breakfast. I'm used to them. I tend to forget. Come on."

They moved down the narrow, curving staircase to the floor below and into the sunny kitchen, which looked out over the backyard through a wall of windows. There was coffee already made, sitting over a low flame on the stove. The smell of it was suddenly magic on the morning air.

"That picture," she asked, when he had poured two cups. "Did you—did you find the teddy bear there, or put it there?" They sat at the table, looking out over the snow-covered yard. The sun was warm, and the thick covering of snow was already beginning to melt at the edges.

A tiny smile brushed his mouth. "I found it there."

"Do you ever...I mean, someone told me once he'd seen a photographer set up a completely phoney scene...that child at the Berlin wall, releasing a white dove, someone told me they'd been there, the photographer had bought the dove and paid the kid to let it go."

Ben rubbed the back of his neck. "Yup," he agreed.

"Do you do that kind of thing a lot?"

"I never do that kind of thing."

"Why not?"

"Because I take pictures of war, and war is always uglier than anyone's imagination could make it, including my own. There are always plenty of potential pictures. Far too many. Everything you look at is heartbreaking."

She sat in silence, drinking her coffee and watching him. He was relaxed this morning, leaning back in his chair, his hair ruffled and glinting in the sun as he looked out at the day. Yet underneath she sensed the potential coil of mental muscle. He was like a big cat, looking lazy but capable of instant reactions.

"Thank you for last night," she said softly. "You have such a nice, comfortable bed, I'm sorry to have put you out."

He turned his head, and his eyes lazily found hers and fixed her so that she couldn't move. He smiled. "Anytime," he said. "Anytime."

9

Marie popped out into the hall as soon as she heard the elevator door open at ten o'clock that morning.

"Oh, Sam, there you are! Where on earth have you been?" she demanded by way of greeting.

Sam blinked in surprise and said hello. Marie was protective, but she wasn't nosey. Sam unlocked her apartment door and ushered the frail child inside. "Can I feed you?" she begged. "You look starving."

"I am starving. Yes, I'll have a coffee if there's one going. Listen—" she couldn't restrain herself "—Justin telephoned me last night from Germany. I almost died."

Sam blushed. She felt the heat burn up from her throat all the way to her forehead. Marie awkwardly looked away. Furious with herself for blushing for no reason and giving her friend entirely the wrong impression, Sam turned away and began fussing with the coffee-maker. "Why on earth did he call? What did he say?"

Marie moved over and sat at the table, then reached out and pulled up the venetian blind, so that the sunlight came flooding into the friendly little room. "He was trying to find you. He tried to call you here, but you'd forgotten to turn on your answering machine.

So he called me. Apparently you'd told him about last Sunday, and he thought maybe you were with me again.''

"With you *again?* What do you mean, again? I wasn't with you last Sunday night, you threw me out in the middle of *Casablanca!*" Sam said in mock indignation.

Marie smiled willingly, but the joke fell flat because she was simultaneously frowning with worry. "Yeah. I told him I thought you were at your friends' place for dinner—Mercedes—Sam, I'm sorry, I really did think that's where you were."

Sam made a face. "Yeah, I was booked, but—"

"I'm real sorry. He phoned them, and then he called me back to say you weren't there after all, and if I heard you come in would I ask you to call him."

Sam cursed. This was all she needed. Put in the position of having to explain the unexplainable. That was her first reaction. Her second was, "Why was he doing all this? It's not like Justin. What did he say?" Suddenly she wondered if he had remembered the date, remembered that it was a terrible anniversary for her, and had called to comfort her. Her heart softened instantly. Of course she shouldn't have gone to Ben's. She didn't need to, when she had Justin.

Marie made a sad face. "His sister is in the hospital, Sam. Overdose or something. From what he said, I don't think his mother took it very well."

All the blood drained from Sam's head, leaving her white, shaking and horrified. "Oh, God, oh, dear God, is she all right? Is she going to be okay?"

"He didn't call me again after midnight."

"How was Simone then? Is it Simone? It must be Simone," Sam babbled.

"I thought he said Mona."

"Moan. They call her Moan. She used to be a whiny kid and it stuck, Justin says."

Marie didn't bother commenting on that. "He didn't really know how she was. I think he was hoping you could go down to the hospital and get some information. Veronica didn't go or something, I didn't really get the whole picture."

Sam took the number of Justin's hotel in Berlin from her, and pressed the buttons with trembling fingers, but Justin had already checked out. He must be flying back early. The McCourt phone was busy. "Did he say which hospital?" she asked Marie.

"Toronto General," Marie said.

"Hi," Sam said quietly, bending to kiss her. "How're you doing?"

Simone smiled weakly as she sat up to accept the bunch of pink and white roses. "Oh, they're pretty, Sam. Thanks. It's nice of you to come. No one else has."

"How are you feeling?" Sam asked again.

"Pretty awful. They don't like attempted suicides much, you know. They make it as awful as they can, on the principle that you won't be so silly and demanding another time."

Simone made Marie look like a "before" picture in a weight-loss ad. She was even paler than usual, and far too thin. Sam shook her head and passed her a box of chocolates and some fresh green grapes.

Simone's eyes were damp. "Chocolates, grapes and flowers. You're so nice and normal, Sam. I wish we were like you." She pulled a grape from the bunch and rolled it absently in her fingers, as if she had forgotten what it might be for.

"Justin's caught a flight home, I think. When I phoned, he'd checked out of his hotel."

"He'll be cursing me, I guess. What was he doing over there?"

"An academic conference. It wasn't important. He's already delivered his paper in Venice," Sam said reassuringly.

"Have you spoken to Veronica?"

Sam tried not to avoid her eyes, but failed. "No," she lied. "I couldn't reach her."

Simone smiled. "I guess she gave you an earful about me. She thinks it's just attention-seeking. That's why she won't come down here. She doesn't believe in rewarding negative behaviour. Neither do my grandparents."

There was nothing to say to that, so Sam just made a helpless face. "I guess they don't understand."

"You know what? Are you engaged to Justin, Sam?"

"Yes, I am. We weren't going to tell anyone till the ring was ready, though."

"Well, you know what? I like you, I like you a lot, but I hope you don't marry Justin. You're too real to marry into this family, Sam. You should think it over. I'd love to have you for a sister, but it wouldn't be for very long anyway," she said with a calmness of purpose that froze Sam. "So I can talk without any selfish motive. Don't do it. They'll take your blood and drain it all away till you're just like Veronica. I haven't got any blood left, that's my problem. Don't let them do it to you, Sam."

* * *

Justin came straight to the hospital from the airport, meeting Sam there. "What a little fool!" he exploded to Sam, before going into Simone's room. "What does she think she's doing?"

Sam looked at him. "Isn't it obvious?"

"Trying to kill herself! What nonsense. Of course she doesn't mean it!"

"Who told you that?"

"I don't need to be told! She's always used extreme attention-getting behaviour, all her life."

"But nobody ever gave her the attention she wanted?" Sam asked gently. She had always been uncomfortable with the family's casual, mocking treatment of "Moan".

He frowned in utter incomprehension. "Of course she got all the attention she needed! This is just stupid, childish...! I almost didn't come back, but..."

Sam was angry suddenly. "But what if she'd succeeded, right? There'd be a funeral to arrange. I suppose you had to think of that."

"Don't be ridiculous, Sam!"

"It wasn't a game, Justin. She took enough to kill a horse. She was only found in time because a friend had her bag snatched with her house keys in it and turned up on the doorstep at midnight asking to be put up for the night because she was afraid to go home."

It stopped him, for the first time. "Veronica didn't tell me that." Then he rallied. "She tried it once before, you know. But she made sure we would find her in time."

She knew she was hearing Veronica talking. Justin was more sensitive than this; he was just dreadfully shocked and trying not to face what it would mean to him to lose his sister. "The more often someone tries, the more likely she is to succeed, Justin. If you go in there blaming her now, be prepared for the consequences."

"All right, darling," he said, bending to kiss her. "I'm sure you're right. I'll treat her with perfect tenderness."

"Ben?"

There was a pause so brief she wasn't sure it was one. "Hi, Sam," he said. His voice was deep and firm, and already she felt everything was going to be fine.

"Ben, something's happened."

"I can hear it in your voice. What's up?"

"Justin's sister took an overdose last night, and Justin tried to call me from Berlin, and of course I wasn't in. I wasn't in all night. Tonight he asked me where I was, and I said . . . It would have been impossible to explain about you, Ben, and—"

And so she had lied. It had shocked her when the lie came off her tongue, but she told herself she couldn't possibly have embarked on the truth, not with Justin already so worried about Simone. She had never lied to him before, but she hadn't been able to see any other way out.

"And what did you say?" he asked lazily. "Am I an old girlfriend he's never happened to meet?"

"I said I stayed the night at your parents' place because I had drunk too much to drive," she said in a rush, hating her own weakness.

He laughed. "Much better than a girlfriend."

"Please don't make a joke of it! I hated lying to him, it's awful. I've never lied to him before."

"Nothing happened, Sam, have you forgotten? I spent the night in the studio. Did you imagine I had come in during the night and seduce you in your sleep?"

She felt the heat in her cheeks. "There was no way to explain to him! How was I going to tell him about our scam on Miranda? I couldn't start all that explanation! It sounds so ridiculous."

"No, of course you couldn't," Ben agreed mildly.

"Ben..." She hesitated. "Ben, would you... if it came to that, would you lie for me?"

"Of course," said Ben.

She heaved a sigh of relief. "You would?"

"We can't have you losing a rich fiancé because of my mother's fetish for chesty blondes," said Ben. "But is it likely to come to that?"

"The thing is—of course Justin didn't know I knew you. Now he wants to meet you. If I say no, it'll seem odd. Would you be willing to have dinner at my place with Justin?"

"Why not bring him along to Sunday dinner with the family? Won't that make a better alibi?"

"Are you kidding? How would we explain it all to your family? They think I'm dating you!"

"Oh, so they do," Ben agreed calmly. "All right, then."

"Would Thursday next week be all right?"

"It's fine."

"The thing is, I kind of let him think I'd been a friend of your family for ages."

"I'll pretend I've known you since you cut your teeth. Want me to bring a date?"

She heaved a sigh of relief. "Oh, could you?"

"Nothing easier. Thursday night, then."

* * *

"Very pleased to meet you," Justin said earnestly to Ben. "I admire your work very much. I had no idea you and Sam were friends."

"We go back a long way," Ben said.

He bent to kiss Sam's cheek, and she was so grateful to him she had an impulse to put her arms up and hug him. "Where's the ring? I thought you were supposed to have it by now," he asked.

"Oh, you know about that? We're saving it for her birthday," Justin said. "My family is throwing a little party, and she's going to have it then."

His family had expressed their own brand of discreet approval at the announcement, Veronica being so quick with hers that Sam had fleetingly wondered whether *she* had known of the engagement before Sam did.

Ben looked at Justin, grinning. "I see. Does this mean you're not officially engaged till then?"

"Of course not," said Sam, while Justin said, "Well, in a manner of speaking, I suppose."

Sam raised her eyebrows, but Justin didn't notice.

"When's your birthday, Sam? How much time have I got?" Ben asked.

"You know when my birthday is," she chided him gently. "Two weeks. You'd have to be a very fast mover."

"But I have a head start, don't I? I've known you lots longer than Justin."

"Should have made your move before this, then," Justin said comfortably.

They had moved into the living room, and Justin was pouring drinks. Ben's date was a blonde named Deirdre who was a dead ringer for a Barbie doll. Ben caught Sam gazing at her in amazement, and grinned at her, so that she had to bite her lip to keep from laughing. "Where do you find them?" she mouthed at him.

"What's that, darling?" Justin asked, handing Deirdre a glass of fizz.

Sam coughed violently. "Nothing. Something in my throat." Behind Justin, Ben was shaking his head.

"We've met before, you know," Deirdre took the opportunity to say to Justin. "But I don't suppose you remember me."

"We have?" Justin smiled gently at her. He was well used to adoring females. "Were you in one of my classes?"

She shook her head, sipping the champagne, which was Justin's contribution to the evening. "Uh-uh. I was at school with your sister Simone. Havergal. I used to be over at your parents' place sometimes when you were there." She smiled, and made a face. For someone so gorgeous, she was amazingly unself-conscious. When she made a face, she actually made a face, without worrying about whether it would distort her pretty expression or give her wrinkles in future. "I had the most awful crush on you. We all did. But I know you never noticed me once."

She took a deep breath. She was wearing a white wool dress with a high neckline that had a teardrop cut-out over the cleavage, and it was quite a cleavage. Even Sam was riveted by it.

"I must have been blind," he said gallantly.

"No, I had acne," Deirdre said simply. "And I was fat."

Well, no one could call her fat now. And the acne had left her skin without a blemish. And it was pretty clear that that old crush wasn't entirely dead.

"No one would ever guess it," Sam said, for something to say, because the conversation was just at the point of drooping.

Justin smiled reassuringly at Sam as he handed her a glass. Deirdre's charms were engagingly obvious, but Sam, he reminded himself, had class. "Go for class in a wife, Justin," Veronica had always said. "It lasts. Never marry a woman who would do better as a mistress."

"There you are, my darling," he said placatingly.

Sam was a little irritated by his attitude. What made him think she might be jealous of Deirdre? She seemed like a perfectly nice woman, and entirely without malice, and Sam was inclined to like her.

Sam chatted to Deirdre about Simone for a few minutes—not mentioning what had just happened, because Deirdre seemed unaware of it—while the men discussed war. She could tell somehow—she wasn't sure how—that Ben did not want to talk about his work. But she supposed Ben was capable of changing the subject if he wished.

"Shall we eat?" she said, when the conversation had got well warmed up, and led them to the table.

She had kept the meal simple, spaghetti with pesto sauce from her local deli, and salad, with salami and marinated asparagus to start. Sam had no separate dining room, and she had set the table in the kitchen with a checked cloth and candle in a bottle, to give it an Italian trattoria flavour. But somehow it didn't quite work. She realized that Justin would have been happier with something more elegant, a background that flattered his good points. He wanted to impress Ben Harris, and a mock-seedy Italian bistro wasn't his setting. Sam couldn't understand, seeing it so clearly now, how she had come to make such a basic error.

"Not *quite* Italy, darling," Justin started by saying, when he saw the table. "You should have remembered I've just come back from the real thing."

It wasn't at all like Justin to put her down in front of other people like this. "I didn't mean it to be Italy," she pointed out mildly. "I meant it to be an Italian bistro in Toronto."

"Quite another animal," Justin agreed.

"I think it's cute," said Deirdre. "And I'm starving."

Sam began to see what Ben saw in her. Aside from the obvious, of course.

Ben was thoroughly at home. Either he would be at home anywhere, or she had unconsciously chosen *his* setting. He looked like a thirties intellectual who would sit up all night discussing ideas over cheap wine and cigarettes and then go off in the morning to fight the Spanish Civil War.

"I thought you were in Germany," he observed to Justin, again displaying how much he apparently knew of Sam's life and loves. Sam hoped he wouldn't end by going overboard on the subject.

"Only very briefly, I'm afraid. I'd been delivering a paper in Venice and drove up to Germany for another conference. But I didn't stay."

"How is your sister?"

Sam tried to catch his eye across the table, but failed.

"Oh, you heard about that?" Justin glanced at Sam as though this was a piece of family history he would have preferred to keep quiet.

"Sam said she was taken ill suddenly the other night while Sam was at my parents' place."

"Was she? Simone?" Deirdre asked. "What happened? I'm so out of touch with everyone these days."

"She's absolutely all right. Not a thing wrong with her. Simone's always been a problem of one sort or another," Justin said. Sam knew it was only because he didn't want the news to get out, but she wished he could have sounded less cold. Ben was watching him with a steady look that made her uncomfortable.

The conversation got over that little hiccup. Ben was so easy; it all flowed.

He was eating with his fingers, a habit Justin had firmly broken Sam of. He would reach out a hand as he was talking, roll up a slice of salami around a stem of asparagus and eat it like a sausage roll, all the while fixing Justin with a gaze that seemed casual and yet...it was as if he drew out of Justin, not the person he usually was, nor the one he wanted to be seen as, but—who? Someone a good deal less attractive than either. He was coming across tonight as rather smug, much more like Veronica than Sam had ever seen him.

"Sam says you have one of my father's sculptures in your living room. How do you find living with it?" Ben asked.

Justin was startled. "Your father?" he repeated, almost condescendingly. "No, the only thing of note I have is a Michael Welsh. My mother is very fond of his stuff. Difficult, of course, but a genuine world-class talent." He glanced at Sam indulgently. "Really, darling, you should be beyond a mistake of that nature by now.''

Sam thought, with sudden inconsequence, that she would not want to see a picture of Justin that had been taken by Ben.

''Michael Welsh is Ben's natural father,'' she said quietly, since presumably he wouldn't have raised the subject if he weren't willing to have it talked about.

Sam couldn't understand why, but Justin was absolutely blown away.

''Really?'' he demanded. He blinked at Ben. ''Your father is Michael Welsh? Why is your name Harris?''

''My parents never married,'' Ben said. ''I was adopted by my mother's husband.''

Of course Justin was too much a man of the world to be shocked by that, or even to notice it. ''How interesting! My mother absolutely loves his work. You must tell him,'' Justin said, as if endorsement by Veronica Taggart was any artist's highest accolade. Yet Sam knew he didn't think like that. ''She can't always get a piece she wants—quite often she has to make do with someone else entirely. But I'm lucky enough to have got his 'Hunger' for the sitting room.'' As if he'd chosen it himself. Sam found herself cringing. Ben was so intelligent. Couldn't Justin see that his eyes saw through this kind of bluster?

''Will you be taking it with you when you move to The Romanoff?'' Ben asked. She was beginning to be shocked by just how much she had told Ben about Justin. Again she tried to catch Ben's eye.

Justin raised his eyebrows, but when it came down to it, he wanted to impress Ben. Or maybe Deirdre. Or both. ''Oh, quite possibly. It will depend on the rest of the decor, of course. You can't put a piece like that just anywhere.''

"No," Ben agreed softly.

"My mother hasn't seen the new space yet. Mind you, it's not mine yet, is it, darling? You're rather jumping the gun a bit, telling anyone about it.''

"Sam and I are old friends. She tells me everything.''

At last she managed to smile a warning at him, but Ben was oblivious.

''I put in an offer that was substantially lower than the asking, of course,'' Justin said, sounding pompous and utterly unlike himself, as though he wanted to impress them with his great financial cunning. ''They've turned it down. I'm waiting a couple of weeks to let them sweat a little before making another offer.''

''I suppose you don't want it very badly,'' Ben observed. This time he did look at Sam, and the implication—to her, at least—was obvious. A little flicker of something like anger was born in her.

''Pour yourself some more wine, Ben,'' she offered, in a tone that made him open his eyes at her.

''Oh, I wouldn't say that. It's a very good space. Good location, too. Yes, we're quite taken with it, aren't we, darling? They're playing hard to get, but I think the agent is in my camp sufficiently to tell me if there were a real threat from another buyer. Anyway, no doubt the other residents would prefer to see it go to a Canadian than to say, another Arab ambassador, and I believe they have some say.''

He said ''a Canadian'', but he meant ''a Mc-Court'', and they all heard it in his voice. Sam dropped her eyes.

"You're a braver man than I am," Ben said. "I don't think I'd risk losing something I wanted by leaving it on the market even for a couple of weeks."

Above Sam's head the eyes of the two men locked for a moment. As far as Ben was concerned, this constituted fair warning, but he could see that Justin chose not to hear.

10

"**I**'m a little late," Sam called down the entry-phone. "Will you wait, or shall I come in my own car?"

"I'll wait," Ben said. "Can I come up?"

She hesitated, without knowing why. "Sure," she said then, and pressed the buzzer. She didn't know why she had hesitated. No reason why Ben shouldn't be in the apartment while she was dressing. She ran and put on a bathrobe over her underwear and went to meet him at the door.

"Hi!" he said cheerfully, leaning down to kiss her lightly. This time not the cheek but the lips, but it was a perfectly casual kiss, and she supposed they were friends enough for that now, after Thursday night.

"So, how did we do?"

She grinned. "Very well, thank you. Justin was tremendously impressed."

"I thought he might be."

She eyed him, looking for irony, but he showed her a face of innocent blandness.

"I'm really grateful, but if you don't want me to keep your family waiting, we'd better talk about it in the car."

On her next dash to the bathroom she noticed that he was at the kitchen table, brooding over the Saturday cryptic crossword puzzle she'd started this morning. "Is there a pen that works in this bunch?" he demanded. In his fruitless search he had created a little pile of useless pens on the table beside the flowerpot.

"Oh—I think I took it to my desk. Look beside the phone," she called.

"What are you saving them for?" he called as she passed into the bedroom again.

She laughed. "I just never get around to tossing them, that's all."

"I see your point. It would take a whole day." A second later she looked up to find him standing at the open bedroom door. He held up a hand filled with a clutch of useless pens. "Now you see them," he said firmly.

"Are you throwing them all out?"

"Well, I'm not taking them to the Royal Ontario Museum."

"Don't make me laugh while I'm putting on my eye makeup," she scolded.

He moved to the kitchen, and she heard the crash of pens into the garbage bin.

"Thank you. You've taken a great load off my mind. I couldn't do it myself."

"Ben's Disposal Engineers. We Never Sleep." Ben found the one working pen by her computer and returned to the puzzle. "Did you fall asleep in the tub?"

"I've had Justin's sister Simone here all afternoon. We went for brunch and then she just needed to talk. I thought I wouldn't make it tonight, but she had a date with your friend Deirdre."

"Deirdre said she'd be calling her."

"I think Deirdre will be good for Simone. She's so nice, isn't she?"

"Very nice," Ben agreed.

"Why don't you marry her?"

"We have agreed that we would not suit," Ben said, in the tones of an Anthony Trollope novel. Sam laughed, feeling lighthearted suddenly after a long wearing day, and began to pull her dress over her head.

"'Interval' is wrong," she heard him call when she had resurfaced from the soft black folds.

"Can't be," she protested.

"Has to be. Otherwise ten down doesn't fit."

"What's ten down?" she rushed into the bathroom and began to damp her hair with her hands, curling tendrils around her face.

"'Bitter'". There has to be an *R* where the *V* is in Interval. Ah."

"Have you got it? What is it?"

"'Integral'. Gap among others not first-class component.'" No wonder you made such a mess of 18 down."

"I lost patience with it." Sam dashed out of the bedroom, dressed in a loose, full-skirted black dress with a roll-neck collar. "Can you fix this? The zipper's stuck."

Ben obediently stood up as she turned her back. She drew her hair to one side, and then he was looking down at the bare curve of her neck. For a second he stood there, not moving, and then he said, "There's hair caught in it."

She felt his hands against the skin of her neck, and closed her eyes with surprise at the unexpected shock of the connection. She stood motionless, trying not to gasp, enduring it, as Ben wrestled with the lock of her hair and the zipper.

At last it was over, and she let out her breath as she felt the hair come free. "Tha—" she began, and then choked, because what she felt now she knew without question was Ben's mouth against the back of her neck.

She closed her eyes again. "Ben," she whispered. "Don't, Ben." How was it she could forget this possibility, joke with him like a brother and then so suddenly find that her awareness of him had changed into something so different?

"Sam." He sounded like a man finding water in the desert, and that tone in his voice melted her where she stood. His hand came up to grip her upper arm, his other was in her hair, and his mouth rested softly against the skin under her ear.

They stood like that, caught unmoving in a web of desire, while the blood leapt in their bodies and desire flooded their hearts.

"Ben," she choked. "I'm engaged to be married."

"Not yet," he said desperately. "Not yet." His hands moved then, and he turned her around to face him, and stroked a tendril of hair from her temple.

His eyes were black, gazing into hers, his hand on her arm so firm. He would do whatever she let him do, and then some. "Not yet," he said again. His hand left her temple and slipped possessively into her hair to cup her neck and head. "Sam."

She thought, *This is what marriage is about. It's resisting passing physical attraction for the sake of a stronger bond. If I fail now, I fail forever.* And she managed to turn away her head in time to avoid taking that full, strong mouth on hers.

Again they stood frozen, their bodies close, her head turned away, his lips helplessly against her hair. Then he let her go.

She picked up her bag and coat in silence, and followed him out the door.

The Harrises were planning Christmas these days. "We spend Christmas at the lake," Andy explained. "We've been doing it ever since Matt was born. Ben was three that year, and he was determined there was going to be snow for Christmas. We were afraid there wouldn't be any in Toronto, so we went up there. We've gone nearly every year since."

"So the weekend of the fifteenth for the tree party," Luke was confirming, writing it in his diary. "I sure hope Rebecca can be counted on to make her appearance before then." He looked sternly at Carol. "Speak to her, okay?"

Carol smiled serenely. "Stop worrying. She'll come when she's ready."

"I don't want us being snowbound up there when you go into labour," he persisted.

"Are you sure you'll be here, Ben?" Ella asked.

"Pretty sure."

"Bring warm clothes, Sam, because we do lots of walking in the snow, and bring your skates, too," someone said.

They had simply taken her as part of the family. It broke Sam's heart to have to say, "I'm sorry, Andy, I won't be able to make Christmas." Of course she would be spending Christmas with the McCourts. They would expect it.

Everybody exclaimed and protested. Andy gazed at her in dismay. "Is Ezra coming home for Christmas? Is that it?"

"Yes, probably. He usually does. But that's not—"

"Well, why not ask him to come, too? We'd love to have him, and we'll make room, even with Rebecca. It'll be lots of fun."

Sam shook her head mutely. "I can't. I really can't. I'm so sorry, I'd love to, but—" She bit her lip, horrified to find she was close to weeping, like a disappointed child. She glanced at Ben for support, but he said nothing. He simply looked at her. Why didn't he say something, tell them she couldn't come?

She would have to stop this charade, she realized. They were only treating her as one of them because they thought Ben was serious about her. She would have to tell them that she was engaged to Justin, stop them, and herself, from doing any more dreaming. She might still be a family friend—she hoped so—but they would have to know that she and Ben were not a couple.

But it was beyond her to say it now.

"Come for the tree decorating party, anyway," said Luke. "That's almost as good as Christmas."

"Yes, come for that!"

She looked helplessly at Ben again. Why didn't he say something to get her off the hook?

"Ben, I can see you're going to have to take a stand here," Arthur said, and the room went quiet while Ben and Sam looked at each other, as though the moment held significance for them all.

"Of course she's coming," said Ben.

* * *

In the car, she said to Ben, "We can't go on fooling your family like this. It's not fair."

"Let's not talk about it now," he said.

"Well, when do you want to talk about it? It's my birthday soon. I don't want to go on with it. We're living a lie, and they're accepting it. I feel like a cheat, Ben."

"Do you? There are ways out of that."

She didn't know what he might mean by that. She said, "What are we going to say?"

"Don't you think you're making a mountain out of a molehill? They've accepted you into the family. So what? I haven't told them we're thinking of marriage, and they know better than to expect it."

That was true, of course. They must have seen dozens of women come and go at Sunday dinners over the years. She said, "Would they treat anyone you were seeing at the moment the same way?"

He paused. "Not quite as warmly, perhaps. They like you for yourself. What's wrong with that?"

"They know we're not serious? They're not treating me this way because they think . . . ?"

She let it fade off.

"They don't think anything. They like you and like your company. And you like them. Or maybe I'm wrong. Is that what you're gently trying to tell me— that you're tired of these loud family get-togethers after all that discreet arty stuff at the McCourts?"

"No!" She glared at him in the darkness, her green eyes sparkling with emotion. "That's not what I mean at all! But it seems to me they—I mean, why are they trying to include me, and even Ezra, in all your Christmas plans?"

"Why wouldn't they?"

There was something in his tone. She said, "You mean your mother isn't pushing you to marry me?"

Ben laughed. "My mother pushes me to marry anyone within reach. It doesn't mean anything. I thought you knew that."

She sighed heavily. She knew there was something wrong, something he wasn't saying, but if it was true that his family's approval of her didn't depend on a belief that she would be related to them in the future, wouldn't it be pointless to make an issue of it now, when it might mean she never saw them again?

"But..."

"If you're worried about me trying to kiss you again, all I can say is, it's a perfectly natural impulse, but I'll try to restrain myself if you insist. Anyway, I'm going out of town tomorrow, so—"

"You *are?*" she protested, forgetting everything else as sudden, unexpected fear shot through her. "Oh, Ben, where?"

"Various parts of Europe. I—"

Her heart was thumping horribly. "Are you going to be on a battlefield?" she whispered. "Where?"

He was silent while he brought the car to a standstill at a stop sign. Then he looked over at her, a dark, indescribable expression in his eyes that made her heart beat very fast.

"Are you?" she insisted, dreading the answer.

"Only very ancient ones. We're doing some location shots for the series," he said at last.

She knew that he was producing a television series on war throughout history. Relief poured violently through her, and in its aftermath she discovered she was trembling. "I don't know how your mother stands it," she whispered.

"Sam," he began, but a car horn sounded behind them, and he turned instead to pull away. They drove in a curious silence after that, Ben staring ahead at the road with an unreadable expression on his face.

When he pulled up at her door, he turned. "The family will expect you next Sunday, even without me. Please go."

"Oh, Ben, are you sure this is the best way?"

"Look at it this way. If they *are* hoping you'll marry me, the worst time to break the truth to them is going to be before Christmas, isn't it? They're already planning on your participation, at least at the tree decorating. It'll spoil things now, if you're not there. It's bad enough that you can't be with us at Christmas, without telling them it's because you're engaged to someone else. Will you leave things as they are until after the holiday?"

When he put it that way, she couldn't argue. Sam took a deep breath. "All right," she said, feeling exactly like a criminal who had got a reprieve. The truth was, it would hurt her more than his family to miss that Christmas tree party.

The truth was, her heart was singing. She was afraid to ask it its reasons.

Her birthday fell on a Saturday. She slept in that morning, and awoke feeling groggy and depressed. When she went to the bathroom she discovered she had her period, and almost wept with vexation. She was often a bit low on the first day of her period, but not usually as low as this. And tonight was her birthday-cum-engagement party at the McCourts.

Well, she would just get through it. She wished Justin hadn't insisted on a public display over the engagement and the ring, but it was too late to protest now. She wished she had his ring on her finger, wished she didn't have the nagging feeling of things unfinished. She wanted to know that it was certain. She wanted the decision over with.

There were three birthday cards in her mailbox that morning, all from different Harrises, and she added them to the collection she had been receiving all week, on her coffee table. None from Ben, she noted. But he was still out of town.

She dressed carefully that evening, needing a lot of time over her makeup because she looked absolutely haggard. She wore her red jersey dress; it wasn't very dressy, but it was flattering, and at least it gave her a bit of colour. She supposed all the McCourts and their friends would be very smart. Probably Justin would expect her to wear her black spaghetti-strap, but she would be cold in that, and her spirits were too low for her to carry it off with poise.

It was Hair from Hell Night, she discovered. Her hair just refused to be put up, thick tendrils determined to escape, all in the wrong places, and falling flat. Over the next half hour she got more and more irritated with it. Tonight of all nights Justin would want her to look chic and smart.

"Damn you!" she screeched after the third attempt, pulling out the band and all the pins that weren't usually necessary. What a day to have her period. If her *hair* put her on the verge of furious tears, how on earth would she get through the evening?

I've seen people who were under daily bombardment, starving and freezing and drinking putrid wa-

ter, make the decision to get married, she heard the voice in her head. But she angrily shook the thought away. Presumably the least of your worries when you got engaged in a city under bombardment was what your prospective in-laws and their friends would think about it.

The doorbell rang. Oh, God, and she was sure she had another half hour at least! Oh, Justin would kill her! She dashed to the entryphone and pressed the buzzer without answering so that he had to come in. She would tell him when he got upstairs what the problem was. Tonight she simply couldn't handle the pressure of Justin deciding to wait for her in the car. She unlocked the door and fled back to the bedroom.

"Damn, damn, damn!" she shouted as the fourth attempt began instantly to go awry. "Come in!" she called when the knock came, and as the door opened, "I'm sorry, I'm late and I just can't help it. My hair won't do a damn thing!"

"Well, it'll sure turn a man on," said a slow, warm voice at the bedroom door, and she whirled.

"Ben!" she cried. "You're back!" Her heart was racing, and just like that the smoke cleared, and the world wasn't hell anymore. She rushed and wrapped her arms around him, feeling as relieved as if he'd returned safe from war.

"I am," he agreed. He was wearing a dark brown leather flight jacket, icy cold to the touch, a white scarf and loose trousers, his craggy face lightly flushed with cold, his black hair tousled, and he looked just like a romantic lead in a war movie. She smiled at him, delighted just to have him there.

"You mustn't smile like that, my beauty, at a man who has promised not to kiss you," he said softly, and wrapped her in his arms.

But it wasn't a passionate kiss, for all that the coldness of his lips caused a little shivering ricochet to chill her skin, like an ice shower, to her toes. It was the sweet, loving kiss of a man glad to be home. She put up her hands to his face when he let her go. "You're cold," she said.

"It's a cold night." He lifted a hand to her chin and tilted it, gazing down at her face in uncomfortable scrutiny. "This is the big night, I take it."

"That's right," she said, pulling away. "In fact, I thought you were Justin, come to pick me up. What time is it, anyway?" Babbling with nerves, though there was no reason for nerves.

"Ten after seven."

"Oh, thank God for that! I've still got twenty minutes to make this damned hair work!"

"I told you, it works on me just as it is." He grinned down at her with a smile full of tricky messages.

"Justin likes me to wear it up."

His thick eyebrows rose. "He does? Why?"

She didn't answer, but started trying to braid it. If a chignon wouldn't work, a French braid would have to do.

"Pretty symbolic stuff," said Ben with a grin. "Are you sure you want to go through with the engagement?"

"What's symbolic about it?" she demanded. "I look better with my hair up."

"No, you don't. You look more controlled, which is something else entirely. If he's curbing your exuberant hair now, what will he do with your personality?"

Now she was irritated, when a minute ago she'd been feeling pleasure in his company. "Will you get out of here?" she said testily. "He'll be here soon, and I want to get ready."

"Don't you even want to know what I brought for your birthday?"

"Did you get me a present for my birthday?" she demanded in childish delight, putting down the comb.

"Of course I did."

"Oh, you didn't have to do that! What is it?" she babbled, making him laugh. He reached into his jacket and pulled out a large jeweller's case and handed it to her, and Sam, eager and excited, reached up to kiss his cheek before snapping it open.

Then she went still. Between her hands, on a bed of white satin, lay the most beautiful thing she had ever seen. Crude, barbaric, crafted in thick gold, it was a necklace fit for a princess. A warlord's daughter.

"Oh, Ben," she breathed. "Oh, how beautiful! Oh, where did you find it?"

"It's a reproduction of an ancient Celtic piece," he said, shrugging out of his jacket and dropping it on the bed.

"It's far too expensive, Ben!" she protested. "I— oh, it's so lovely, but I can't take it!"

"Not expensive at all," he said with a grin, lifting it out of the case and moving behind her. "I bought the gold-plated version. Were you imagining it was solid gold?"

She smiled at him in the mirror. Of course it wouldn't be gold. How foolish of her. As he lifted his arms over her head and placed it around her neck she pulled her hair out of the way and bent her head, waiting till it was fastened to look at herself.

Then the expectant smile left her face.

It transformed her. With her hair flowing everywhere, with the rich, deep red of her high-collared dress, she looked like an illustration from fantasy. Her cheekbones seemed to gain prominence; the faint exotic slant of her green eyes was more pronounced. She looked wild and untamable, the warrior queen of an ancient people. All she needed was a sword and a cat familiar.

Her eyes met his in the mirror. "Oh, Ben, isn't it fantastic?" she breathed.

"Oh, yes," he said, his voice just a little rough-edged, as though it was not what he wanted to say. "You'll knock 'em dead."

She laughed at that. "Will I? I'll certainly convince them I'm not right for Justin."

"No?"

"I—they'll all be so—I'd be so out of place." She went on smiling, but now there was a lump in her throat, as though there was something to be said, or felt. She swallowed.

"Beauty, you *are* out of place. Isn't that why Justin chose you? Because you're different? I suppose he could have had his pick of a dozen clones of his mother."

Was that why he had chosen her? She had never really thought before how different she was from the McCourts. She had seen *them* without really seeing herself in comparison. Perhaps it had taken this necklace to make her do that. To show her herself. She looked at the woman in the mirror again.

"Is this me?" she asked.

Ben only blinked at her, like a cat, meeting her eyes in the mirror. Then, "Is it?" he asked her back.

"You're the one who knows the answer to that." She heard urgency in his voice, as if he were trying to tell her something.

She stared at her reflection. Maybe it was. Maybe she really had this inside her, primitive energy, deep feminine sexuality. The world seemed suddenly so strange, as though she'd been seeing it through a mirror up to now and her eyes hadn't quite adjusted to the new way of seeing things.

"Well, I know one thing," she said. "If it *is* me, tonight certainly isn't the night to announce the fact."

He watched her, and she added defensively, "I don't always have to be telling people who I am, you know!"

"No," he agreed levelly. "There may be lots of reasons to hide your light. But if you choose not to be yourself tonight out of fear, then be prepared not to survive marriage with Justin McCourt. Because though he may have chosen you because you are different, he is a man who will nevertheless devote himself to changing you."

With a suddenness that startled her, she was angry. She rounded on him, almost shouting. "Why did you do this? What are you trying to prove, coming in here ten minutes before my party and spoiling everything?"

"Not everything," he stated dryly. "Your hair, if you remember, was already being disobedient when I came in. It, at least, has a mind of its own."

"And I don't?" she demanded furiously.

He grinned. "Beauty, when you shout at me like that, how could I accuse you of not having a mind of your own?"

Something terrible was happening inside her, but she didn't know what it was, only that it was driving her to furious frenzy. "What do you know about it?" she shouted. "What do you know about love, or marriage, or any of it? You're terrified at the thought! You don't know anything about it!"

The smile left his face, and he looked suddenly drawn, and she knew he was angry. "I know this," Ben said, as if goaded beyond endurance. He was an adversary now, his hands reaching out for her before she could stop him, pulling her bodily against him. "I know this," he repeated, his arms unbearably tight around her, his eyes black as he stood looking into her face for a moment during which her heart leapt and pounded in her chest as if fighting to escape the bondage of her ribs.

Then his grip gentled, his hand came up and buried itself in her hair, and the firm strong mouth was inexorable as it came down to find her own.

She had no defenses against the fire that burned through her blood and nerves, against the purely physical passion that swept her. No way to stop the cry of desire and need in her throat, stop her eyes closing, her lips parting under his, her arms' convulsive movement to encircle him and draw him closer.

Then she pushed him away, forcing him to let her go, and they each stood shaken, breathless, searching for calm.

He looked at her for a moment. "No?" he asked dryly.

"What does it prove?" Sam demanded harshly, her breasts heaving, scarcely able to speak for lack of air. "Marriage doesn't mean there's no such thing as temptation."

He barked a laugh without humour. "Temptation? Is that what you call it?"

"What do *you* call it?"

He went on looking at her, his eyes black with an emotion that could only be anger. "You know what I call it. You don't want to hear me say it, do you? It would disturb your ordered, safe little life."

She did *not* want to hear it, if what he was going to say was that passion was more important than marriage, that a fling with him was worth a whole future with Justin. It was not, but if he said it, she might believe him, might believe for a crucial few hours, or days, or weeks, that the experience he was offering her was worth any price.

If all the price could be paid beforehand . . . but she knew that the real cost would come later, when he left her alone and regretting. She would have nothing then, not even half the loaf.

"Yes, I think it would," she said stonily.

He turned, picked up his jacket, and went out.

11

In the end she wore the black spaghetti-strap dress, because Justin said the red simply wouldn't do, not for tonight's star attraction. And he didn't mind waiting while she struggled to get her hair perfect, because it would be quite all right for them to arrive late. Of course she didn't wear any rings, and heavy silver earrings and a bracelet would later complement the white gold of her engagement ring.

When she was ready at last, Justin eyed her approvingly. "You really do have a certain flair, darling," he said, bending to kiss her safely on her bare shoulder so as not to spoil the smooth finish of her makeup.

All night she was torn between a desire to weep and one to scream. She didn't know what was wrong with her, except that a) she had her period, and b) Ben Harris was a jerk. But champagne, and there was plenty of that, should have lightened both those weights on her spirit, and that it didn't was the mystery.

No one seemed to notice, but then, the McCourts were not a noticing family. With the exception, perhaps, of Simone. Her eyes darkly shadowed, her pale hair newly cut short around her head, a thin blue satin slip of a dress over a thin white body, and boots on her feet, she looked heart-rendingly pathetic. "You didn't listen to me," Simone said, her eyes burning holes through Sam. "You're going to do it, aren't you?"

"Simone, I love him."

"I bet you don't. You're blinded by all the charm, but you sure don't look happy, do you? He's not a lovable boy, my brother, when you get to know him. I nearly did it tonight, just to save you from this family."

"What?" Sam breathed, horrified.

"I figured not even the McCourts could go ahead with the party if their daughter had just entered the gates of Lethe."

"I'm glad you didn't, Simone," Sam said quietly.

"Yeah, well, you've been so kind to me lately that if I did it now I figured you'd feel guilty, and I didn't want that. I mean, you've done all anybody could, Sam, and I appreciate it. So when it happens, I don't want you to feel guilty, okay? I mean, I don't want anybody to feel guilty, I just want out. But they won't, and you might. I really mean it. It's not your fault, it's just that you—came along too late." She was speaking in a dry, almost businesslike tone that scared Sam much more than emotion and tears would have done.

"Simone, please don't kill yourself," Sam said, on the point of tears. Everything seemed so futile, on a night when she should be so happy.

"Yeah, you see? You can say that." She sipped her drink. "My mother wouldn't dream of saying it."

"Well, I am saying it. You will kill me if you kill yourself. I'm looking forward to having you for a sister."

"If it didn't mean Justin being your husband, I'd love to have you for a sister, too. Why don't we just settle for being friends?" She looked anxious suddenly, for the first time. "Sam, if anything happened between you and Justin—I mean, I hope it will, except—could we be friends anyway, you and me?"

Sam leaned forward and kissed the thin white cheek. "Yes, of course we can, Simone."

A hand clasped her wrist. "Promise me?"

"I promise. Now you promise me."

"Really? It really means something to you?" A spark entered her eyes for the first time, a very faint spark, but something to give Sam hope.

"It means a lot to me. Promise. Find another way out, Simone. You have so much to offer. I know you can find another way if you try."

Simone's eyes left hers as she thought it over. "All right. I promise."

They smiled at each other. It was only much, much later that Sam realized she hadn't protested that of course nothing would happen to break off her engagement to Justin.

Justin's father made the announcement as the guests all stood around in a circle, and then Justin put the ring on her finger at last, and the diamond glittered very satisfyingly, he thought, under the lights, and the ring was just different enough to make them admiring when he said it was his own design.

She had thought she would feel better once the ring was on her finger, thought she would feel that everything was decided. But she didn't. She was still waiting, but for what, she didn't know. The ring was there on her finger; she was engaged officially now, but— she was still unsettled.

Sam tried to avoid Ben and the Harrises after that night, cancelling Sunday dinner by pleading pressures of work for two weeks running, but it wasn't possible to avoid going to the hospital when Rebecca was born, just a little later than expected, the following Tuesday.

The baby had soft curling hair, and the bluest of blue eyes, and she looked around her as though she had found her journey here an adventure and was curious about her new environment. Sam was watching Carol and the baby look at each other with delight, her throat unexpectedly tight, when Ben came into the room.

She looked at him wordlessly, trying to smile but failing, remembering that last scene in her apartment. She looked, feeling that there was something she should know, something she should understand, but like a baby reaching for smoke, she couldn't grasp it.

He nodded at her, his eyes dark, but neither Luke nor Carol seemed to notice the tension between them. It was natural that all attention should focus on the little miracle they themselves had provided.

Only Sam noticed the way he looked at her engagement finger, only Sam understood the raised eyebrow when he saw it was bare. She wanted to scream at him that she had taken it off for his sake, for his family, but of course she could say nothing.

"Do you want to hold her?" Carol asked Sam generously, and Sam immediately bent down and took the soft newborn spark of creation into the crook of her arm and smiled down into those questioning blue eyes.

Her hair, loose around her shoulders, fell forward as she bent over the baby, as though shielding them both from harm, and at that moment, unthinkingly, she glanced up at Ben.

His face was stone. She had never seen him look so hard, so cold, and Sam realized that if she had had a question in her heart, that look on Ben's face was all she needed for an answer. She looked away.

"There are three cottages on the far side, ours is the one with the green shutters and roof," Miranda had told her, and she saw it now at its winter best, with the snow deep around it, protected by a semicircle of naked birch and deep evergreen, and the sun shining brightly from a clear sky. It glinted off the stretch of frozen lake before her, and for a moment Sam stood in the clear crisp air, drinking in the quiet and the solitude. Above her head a jet drew two firm white lines high against the empty stretch of blue sky.

She was supposed to phone on her mobile when she arrived, and someone would come to get her on a snowmobile, but it didn't look far, and she wanted a walk in the crisp air after the city. Sam got her bag out of the car, locked up and set off.

There were snowmobile tracks here and there in the lightly drifted snow across the ice, easy to follow, but the distance was further than she had expected, and her fingers and nose were cold by the time she had arrived at the other side.

It was a rambling wooden house with a long covered verandah running into a dock that led straight down to the water's edge, and probably very old— Victorian, by the look of it. Sam climbed the steps onto the dock, where in summer no doubt boats would be moored, but now a snowmobile sat, and walked up towards the house. The closer she got, the more protection the house seemed to promise, until the verandah embraced her.

"Sam!" Andy said with a huge smile. "There you are! Did you enjoy the walk? Come in, come in!"

Sam was glowing with cold and with the exercise, and the warmth of the room rushed up around her with welcome. Ella and Carol and Alice came up to kiss and welcome her, too, with the news that the men were all out choosing the tree, Sara had gone with them, and they were just making lunch for the moment the hungry travellers returned.

They were all in a massive kitchen filled with sunlight that streamed through a wall of south-facing windows, and the smells of cooking reminded Sam that she had skipped breakfast. Two infants were sitting in high chairs demanding food, and Rebecca was in a carry-cot on the table, watching all the goings-on with acute interest.

Half an hour later, loud voices and a lot of stamping on the verandah signalled the return of the tree-gatherers, and everyone rushed out into the freezing air to admire the thick, handsome pine.

"But it's beautiful!" Miranda said. "I've never seen such a perfectly proportioned tree."

"You can thank Sara for that," said Jude, a little proudly.

"That's the last time we take any girls along on this expedition!" Matt announced in loud masculine indignation. "Sara kept saying they weren't good enough, and just kept driving us on. We must have looked at every tree in a three-mile radius! I thought we'd get lost in the bush."

They were all laughing. "You guys kept picking trees that were only good on one side," Sara accused.

"Now, Matt, how could you get lost?" Miranda said pointedly. "You know the whole peninsula."

"I do *now*," said Matt, with emphasis.

"It's certainly the best tree we've had for a long time," Alice said, walking around it. "Good for Sara. I think a woman supervisor will have to go along every year."

"Yeah, you guys have always said you found the best there was," Ella chimed in. "I thought all the trees grew one-sided up here. Something to do with the wind."

The men groaned and muttered darkly about injustice.

"Sam's here at last, so now we're complete," Miranda said, in the middle of it all, and Sam went the rounds, with kisses of greeting. They were all laughing and talking as the explorers stamped the snow from their boots and wrestled the tree inside. In the melee no one noticed that it was only Ben whom Sam didn't kiss. She scarcely noticed it herself.

The tree was put in a stand and given water, and then everyone trooped into the kitchen for lunch around the big table. By the time that was over and the dishes cleared away, the sun was already low in the sky, and it was time to light the fire in the sitting room and decorate the house and the proud tree.

"Good God, Mom, what's all this mistletoe?" Luke demanded, opening a bag. "Did you break the bank?"

"Nonsense, Luke," said Andy. "There's no more than usual." Sam caught a warning look that passed between mother and son, but couldn't interpret it.

Luke raised an understanding eyebrow and said with a grin, "Yeah, yeah, you always get too much of everything. We'd be having an orgy if you could have your flower-power way."

"Now, Luke, you know that's ridiculous."

There was wine, mulled wine, sherry and mince tarts to keep them going till dinner, and by then the house looked like a Sunday Supplement photograph of "An Old-Fashioned Christmas." Red velvet ribbon with pine-cones and branches and holly decorated picture frames and the mantlepiece; a huge centrepiece sat on the antique pine dining room table; and mistletoe hung from every single doorway.

Sam was kissed whenever she happened to pass through a doorway, because someone was always standing within reach, but she noticed that Ben was somehow never nearby when she did.

Maybe it was simply because he was overseeing the cooking of the big smoked ham on the barbecue outside the kitchen door, and he was often out of the room, but whatever the reason, Sam was glad of it. Whatever Ben said about his family's expectations, she didn't want to contribute to them. Taking off her engagement ring when she came to see them made her feel like a cheat.

She felt restless without knowing why. She was so happy here with them all, and she was counting this as her real Christmas, because whatever happened in ten days at the McCourts' wouldn't bear much resemblance to any Christmas celebration she'd ever known. It was this kind of celebration that her heart remembered from those long-ago days before her parents' death. Still, she was restless, as if waiting for something that would never happen, someone who would never come.

Perhaps she was missing Ezra. He would have enjoyed this, too.

They ate dinner in the big dining area that led off the sitting room, ham with roast potatoes and peas, and then Miranda disappeared into the kitchen with Ella. After a minute the lights went out, and there was only the glow from the Christmas tree and the fire, and another faint glow, with giggles, coming from the kitchen.

At a cue everyone started singing, "Happy birthday to you..." Then the two women came in, Ella shielding what Andy was carrying with a newspaper until they were inside the dining room, then lowering it to reveal a cake with lighted candles. Sam sang, looking around the table for clues as to whose birthday it was. It was with absolute amazement that she saw Andy stop beside her own chair and set the cake in front of her.

"Happy birthday, dear Sa-am, happy birthday to you," they finished. And then there was clapping, and the lights went on again.

"Make a wish and blow out the candles," Andy told her, but Sam's heart was beating so fast she could hardly draw breath.

"But you, but—" she protested helplessly. "It's so *sweet* of you!"

"Make a wish," someone urged her again.

Ben was almost opposite her across the table, and he was looking straight at her for perhaps the first time today, with a look that said he couldn't stop himself any longer. She was caught by the gaze, and her heart began to thud in slow, expectant beats, not knowing what message was in his eyes, but unable to turn away from it, all the same.

"Make a wish, Sam," he commanded softly, his words hardly audible.

At that her gaze fell, because somehow she had to look anywhere but at him. "It's a lovely cake," she said, to relieve the expectant silence.

A wish. She must make a wish. But what was she to wish for, in this group? The silence extended and extended, and her brain could find nothing it was safe to wish for. At last, remembering the phrase from some long-ago story-book, she thought, *Thou knowest the desires of my heart,* and wished for that, for whatever God knew she really wanted.

Then she gulped air, as if it were crucially important, and blew with all her might, and twenty-six candle flames obediently died.

They had gifts for her, too, nothing expensive, just little friendly presents. A new makeup bag for her purse, a small bottle of a new perfume on the market, a book of travel essays...and from Ben, a box of about a dozen brand-new ballpoint and felt-tip pens, red and blue and black.

She laughed when she saw them, and looked up to smile at him in the memory of that evening...and of the other evening, later, when he had given her a very different gift. Her eyes locked with his again, and she saw for the first time that he was looking so drawn he was almost haggard.

Her heart caught in her throat, but she resolutely dropped her eyes again. Whatever was causing Ben to look like that, it was not her business to comfort him.

"Now what's the significance of *that?*" Matt demanded, beginning to laugh. "Ben, I hand it to you!

You're the only guy I know who could give a girl twenty cheap pens on her birthday and get a look like that out of it!''

"It's a knack," said Ben lightly, and Sam wondered if she was the only one who heard the strain in his voice.

And then the moment passed.

"Of course, we had all this planned for the Sunday after your birthday," Miranda told her later. "We were all very disappointed you couldn't come that night, but this is just as good, isn't it? Belated, that's all."

"It's a long time since I had such a nice birthday party," she said, and then she clapped her hand to her mouth, because it was only two weeks ago that she had celebrated her birthday and engagement at the McCourts'.

"What is it?" Andy asked, but Sam just shook her head. Suddenly she found she was trembling. She stood up, wanting to escape, but not knowing from what. Ben was in the doorway to the hall, leaning against the doorpost, watching the room. As she slipped past him, he turned suddenly, and his arms came around her, and before she could protest he was kissing her.

There had been plenty to drink at dinner, and before, and her head swam crazily as his mouth found hers, so that she had to cling to him for balance. At the touch of her hands on him, his hold tightened, and her head went back into the crook of his arm, and he kissed her as a man might kiss a woman he loved when he was dying, with a kiss where forever was all bound up in one moment. A kiss with all the passion of a lifetime, and years of never-to-be spoken love.

Then he let her go, and strode out of the room, and a moment later she felt a gust of icy air, and heard the bang of a door. Sam fled across the hall towards the bathroom.

"Mom," Luke said lazily into the silence, "where in the *hell* did you pick up that mistletoe?"

12

They played Trivial Pursuit all evening, inevitably in six teams of couples, when the children were all in bed. Sam's brain was in a state of confused upheaval, and Ben didn't seem to be very focused, either. When asked for the capital of former Yugoslavia, he even answered "Sarajevo" instead of "Belgrade", to everyone's surprise. Sam and Ben lost miserably, coming in a distant last with only two pieces in their pie while Matt and Ella sailed home.

"Well, that's not like you, Ben," Arthur said comfortably, as they packed away the game preparatory to going to bed. "That's the first time you haven't won since we got the game, probably."

But the worst was to come, Sam found. Because when Miranda said, "Well, we'd better get that sofa made up for you, Luke," Ben said, *"What?"* with a roar that astonished them all.

Andy turned innocent eyes on her eldest son. "Luke's sleeping on the sofa tonight. Carol says he's too restless a sleeper, and that bed in his room is only a double, you know."

Ben's face was hard and bleak, and he missed the conspiratorial look that passed between Luke and his mother. Carol chimed in, "You have no idea how that guy can aim a kick, and I'm still sort of...a bit sore.

I want the bed to myself. It's not going to put anyone out, is it?''

Sam was mystified until she was shown to her bedroom and discovered that she was sharing it with Ben. The door closed behind them, and she stared at him, her heart thumping uncomfortably. He was looking furious.

"Ben," she said awkwardly.

"I damned well told my mother I'd be sleeping on the sofa tonight!" he said. "She can't have forgotten."

"Isn't there anywhere else?" she whispered.

"Not without one of us freezing to death during the night," he said, rubbing the back of his neck and cursing under his breath, as though looking for a way out when he knew there wasn't one. "The sun porch is okay in summer, and so's the floor. But this place gets damned cold at night. I should have known this would happen. Andy's been looking like a cat all day."

"But . . . why?"

"Because she is pretending to think we are sleeping together as a means of getting us to that point."

"Oh, Ben, are you sure?"

"Sure I'm sure. I'm sorry, Sam, you were right, and I was wrong. We should have made things clear before this." He cursed again.

The room was small, cosy, but with little floor space to spare. Between the foot of the bed and the antique wardrobe there might just be room for a body. He gazed down at it. "I'll sleep in front of the fire in the living room." He pulled open the wardrobe, but there was nothing at all in it, nor in the drawers of the dresser beside it.

He opened the bedroom door and moved down the hall to tap on a door. "Mom," he called. "Where's my sleeping bag?"

The door was opened, and his mother stood there. "Your sleeping bag?" she asked, astonished.

"My sleeping bag. Don't ask questions. It's always in my wardrobe."

"But that's a summer sleeping bag. It isn't warm enough for winter use."

"Never mind that. I want it."

"But, dear, I sent all the sleeping bags to the cleaners yesterday for their annual clean."

"In December?"

"Oh, well . . . you know," she said evasively.

"Yeah, I'm beginning to get the picture," Ben said quietly. "Do you think you could mind your own business, and stop trying to run my life?"

He turned on his heel, leaving her standing there, and Miranda bit her lip. In all his life Ben had never spoken to her in that way. She had never seen him so angry, or so deeply distraught. It must be much worse than she had thought. Maybe it wasn't Ben, but Sam, who was the stumbling block. And yet she'd thought... She toyed for a moment with going to Luke and telling him the game was over, and that he should give up the sofa. But Ben had gone back to his own room and closed the door. Maybe it would come right, after all.

"Can't we just—share the bed without..." Sam didn't finish. Ben leaned over her and put a hand around her throat with a passion held so tightly in check that she was unsure whether he wanted to choke her or kiss her.

"Look," he said with rough violence. "I want you, all right? I want you so bad I can't see my hand in front of my own damn face. Now, as I understand it, you want something very different. If I get into that bed with you, whatever my intentions, sooner or later one thing is going to happen. And if it happens... Are you willing to give up that life you've got planned for yourself? I want to know."

Floodgates opened somewhere, and blood poured into her brain, making her almost black out. She dropped her face and tried to breathe, but under his burning touch, her throat had closed. "Ben," she whispered. "Ben, don't."

She covered her face with her hands, her mind racing as wildly as her blood, her heart half killing her. She whimpered in distress, and at last managed to draw in a shuddering breath, and then another. What was happening to her? What was wrong with her? Of course she was attracted to Ben, she had known that from the beginning, but this was inexplicable. This was like insanity. She had never felt anything like this in all her life. She felt her brain would divide.

"Ben, I'm—I can't. I'm en—"

He said, "If you say that word to me again I will strangle you."

And then he let her go, turned and went out.

She saw him ten minutes later, walking out among the trees, pacing like a wild animal, sometimes stopping to gaze at the house, up at her window, but mostly simply walking up and down, up and down, like some magnificent creature caged and hating it. She watched while all the lights from the various bedrooms went out, one by one, and then there was only the four-square patch of her own light shining down on the snow.

He wanted her. He had said it in a voice that had almost frightened her, and even the memory of it melted her stomach and set all her skin twitching. Was that the answer, then, to the strain she had seen in his face, the look in his eyes?

She thought of the kiss he had given her, in the archway under the mistletoe. She had not been drunk until that touch of his mouth on hers, communicating such desperate hunger that she had nearly fainted.

She had been physically attracted to him from the first moment of seeing him. He had so much animal, masculine presence. But the attraction she had felt then wasn't even a shadow of the dark, burning need she felt now. Their first meeting had been a spark, but now what she felt was a roaring flame that drew her, as if to her destruction. It was as though she looked into the heart of a furnace and could only think of the comfort she would find in its heat, and not of the certain immolation.

She sat at the window, watching, wanting him to come to her and knowing that he must not, knowing she was not free, could make no sign to invite him. That if he did come, if his strength were not equal to his passion, she must repulse him.

She thought of the night of her birthday, and knew that he had been right that night. She should have made love to him before she was officially engaged, so that they could both have got this madness out of their systems. Now it would be a betrayal of Justin. Then— she saw it now for the first time—then Justin had been playing for time, and she, too, had had the right to be certain first.

Her body ached with the effort it took to get up and leave the window, leave the sight of that pacing figure down below that drew her, breast to breast, so that she felt her heart would tear itself from her body and go to him independently.

She sat on the bed and lifted her handbag into her lap. Inside, wrapped in a little velvet bag, she found the diamond and turquoise cluster of the bond that held her, and slipped it on her finger. She stared at it, making it glint in the lamplight. She loved Justin. Didn't she? But then, what was this feeling that drew her to Ben? What was making her wish so desperately that Ben would come to her, in spite of knowing that if he did she must turn him away again? What was making her whole body ache, as if she had been physically beaten, and telling her that he, and only he, would be the salve to soothe the ache?

"Give up that life," he had said, and he was right. He knew her well enough for that. If she made love to Ben tonight, she could not afterwards go back to Justin. She could not cheat, and then pretend nothing had happened. Nor could she make this choice tonight and then ask Justin to forgive her for it. If she chose Ben tonight, she must do it knowing that she chose forever not to marry Justin, knowing that Ben wanted her only for tonight, or for a few weeks, and that at the end of it she would have nothing at all.

She looked at the ring. She had wanted it to answer all her questions, but it hadn't done so. She had thought that this ring on her finger would be her insurance against an unsettled future, would bar her heart against the inexplicable yearning she felt for Ben Harris.

If it had not, could she still believe she loved Justin enough to marry him? Was it right to marry a man when her love for him wasn't strong enough, even in the first weeks of their engagement, to keep her from a feverish, consuming desire for another man, no matter how brief that passion might be in both of them?

She heard a footfall, and then the door opened in front of her, and he stood there, looking white and determined, but no longer haunted. He had made some decision, out there in the night and the cold.

She looked from the ring to Ben's face, and knew that to ask the question she had asked was to answer it. She could not marry Justin when her heart leapt like this in the presence of another man. She could not vow before God and man to forsake all others when her heart told her that, whatever the reason it leapt, it could not forsake Ben.

He closed the door, and then stepped the short step to where she sat on the bed. He lifted her hand and looked at the ring. It was the first time he had seen it, but he could have guessed it would be a cold, bloodless thing. He looked into her face, his own face stripped naked.

"Sam," he said hoarsely, and that was the answer to all the questions, that was the secret that settled everything, her name on his lips. She felt all the disquiet of the past weeks fall away from her. She was not going to marry Justin. That was the answer. Even if she had Ben no longer than this one night, she could never marry Justin.

Sam bent her head under the decision she felt in him, accepting it.

Then he lifted his other hand, and his thumb and forefinger grasped the ring. She looked down at her hands again, and watched in curious detachment as he drew the ring from her finger, not merely to take it off, but formally, as if it were a ritual of significance, and set it beside the lamp.

"You are not going to marry him," he said.

His eyes burning into hers, he drew her up and into his arms, and then, only then, did his control break. He kissed her, his lips burning her, and she put her arms around him and stepped into the inferno of his passion.

And this, she marvelled, was the brand that sealed her fate. Not a ring at all, but Ben's mouth, Ben's hands, Ben's body, marking her forever as his own.

Afterwards, she slept. But Ben did not sleep. He got out of the bed and sat in a chair by the window, watching her in the darkness and tormented by what had been, and what would be. He had said she would not marry the man. But *she* had not said it. She had given in to his passion, but to nothing else.

She dreamt. It was a bright summer day, and there was a church before her, high-steepled and magnificent. She walked up the steps to the wide-open doors, and music played. She looked, and her father was with her, and then she was walking down the aisle with him, and she knew she was a bride, and that he was happy for her.

At the altar a woman stood in bright red vestments, holding a sacred cup. "This is the Alchymical Cup," she intoned, holding it above their heads. She offered it to Sam, and as Sam drank, her head swam. Then she watched as the priestess held the cup out to the bridegroom. "But I can't marry Justin now," Sam thought, curiously prosaic against the mystery of the proceedings.

But when she looked, it was a dark head that was bent over the priestess's cup, and the purple-stained mouth that lifted from it was Ben's mouth. "Ben," she said. "Oh, that's the mystery."

Her heart opened like a flower, and love flowed from it as Ben came close and embraced her with all his being. She had never in her life experienced love like this—full, all-encompassing. Real. "I love you," she said aloud, and opened her eyes.

The room seemed bright, though it was in darkness; she was in the cathedral still, but now Ben was sitting against the window, watching her with eyes that were filled with pain, and she realized that he did not know what she knew, that they were married. She reached out to him. "Come to me," she said, half in the world, half in the dream.

And then he was beside her again, holding her, kissing her with an urgency that matched her own, pressing her to him, hungry, demanding, lost in passion. His body was cold against her skin, and he was half-rough, half-tender, until she was roused from her half-sleep by the touch. "Ben," she said in surprise, marvelling at what she knew.

He heard the surprise, and thought he understood that it was to someone else she had turned in that half-dreaming state, but it was too late then, he was inside her, and if she did not stop him, he could not stop himself. The heat of her enclosed him, and he was drowning in pleasure again, more than he had ever known, all his life long. He thrust and thrust into her, a woman who would be another man's wife, who would never be his own, but who, for this one treacherous moment, when he had worn her down with his need, had agreed to be his.

And it had come to this, that he was taking what she had offered, because, like a starving child, he could not turn away. That he was helpless with passion, that the gods had had their laugh. That when at last he had met the love of his life, the wife his soul craved, she belonged to another man, and he was offered crumbs.

He ate up the crumbs greedily, knowing they must last him a lifetime, brought so low that he was grateful even for this, that, recognizing her mistake, she had not turned away, had not asked him to stop. It was all he needed to be happier than he had ever been, more tortured than he had ever been.

The passion built in them, and then their souls turned to that high altar in the higher world, and the Lady held aloft the golden cup. "And now you are One," she intoned.

What their souls knew, their bodies knew. The ecstasy of Union breathed upon and through them, and joy coursed from the spirit into the body, where it became pleasure, pleasure so profound it made them shudder and cry out, and hold each other as if forever.

He lay beside his Wife in the darkness then, and discovered without surprise that his eyes were wet. He had never cried before at a time like this, but then, he had never loved before.

He had never lost before, a voice told him, but he pushed it aside. That would come later, with memory, and the world.

She found him in the kitchen in the morning, the grey light scarcely lighting the room, with a cup of coffee, looking like a man who had been in hell. "Ben," she said quietly without preamble, "I've got to go back to Toronto."

"You are not going to marry him," he said desperately, knowing that the words meant nothing unless she said them.

She could not tell him that now. Whatever was between them, Justin had this much right over her, that she would say it to him before anyone else. "I have to go," she said doggedly.

He moved a hand, then stopped. "All right," he said.

"I mean *now*."

"I know what you mean. I'm..." But he couldn't say it, couldn't say a feeble word like "sorry" when what he meant was he was dying but nevertheless couldn't wish it undone. He stood up. "All right," he said again.

It was too cold at this hour of the morning to think of walking all that distance over the ice to a cold car. She said, "Will you—" But his face stopped her.

"All right," he said again. "Come on."

He strapped her bag on the snowmobile in silence, and in silence they climbed on and he started the motor with an ugly roar that disturbed the birds and the perfection of the morning. When they were at the other side of the lake, he unstrapped the bag and put it in the car when she unlocked it.

"I guess it shouldn't have happened," he said. "Will you tell him?"

"No," she said, because it would not be necessary.

And then, as he stood there watching, she drove away.

Luke was sitting up on the sofa when Ben returned to the house. "Sorry, Ben," he said softly. "Me and my big mouth, eh?"

"It didn't make any difference to the outcome," Ben said tiredly. But he knew he would be haunted all his life by the thought that if he'd played it a little cooler a little longer he might have won her away from her dreams of money and security and whatever else it was that drew her to a man who was going to destroy all that was best in her.

Sam drove steadily along the icy roads, sorting out what it meant, deciphering all the many clues that she had not understood before now.

It was Ben she loved, with a feeling so unlike what she felt for Justin that she had not been capable of recognizing it for what it was. Ben, who wasn't the marrying kind and who would want her for a month, or two, or three, or perhaps a year...who had tried to resist his passion because she asked him to, because he knew what it would cost her.

She'd had to make her choice knowing that. That was what had prevented her seeing the truth long before. Perhaps that first night, even, it had been her heart talking when she had make the joking proposal.

It was her whole being now, it was everything she was, and yet she hadn't known. All that sense of being unsettled, that desire for Justin's ring on her finger, had been—what had it been? Fear of loving where her love wasn't wanted? Fear of the true passion of her soul, so overwhelming now she seemed to have been born with it?

She had thought Justin was safe, but she was wrong. Only love was safe. She had to go where her heart led, whatever emptiness there might be in the future. She hadn't been cheating on Justin, making love to Ben. She had been cheating on Ben, getting engaged to Justin.

It was so clear, and yet she was terrified. She had come away to think, or so she had told herself, back at the cottage. But she hadn't come away to think. She had come away because she must put it right now, today, while she knew, while the love was stronger than her fear of a future where she would have nothing.

She put her foot down and drove faster.

He didn't like it, and yet she sensed that somehow Justin was relieved. He pretended not to be, he blustered and tried to kiss her, but she was stone, and he wasn't a man to enjoy kissing stone. She set the ring on the top of the sculpture, and it was only then that she heard the noise from the bedroom. With a curious sense of the inevitable, she walked across the room and opened the door.

"Hello, Judith," she said pleasantly. She turned to Justin. "That makes it unanimous, then."

Simone hugged her. "Oh, Sam, I'm so glad! I haven't heard news as good as this for ages! I've been dying to tell you my news, too." She smiled hugely. "I'm going out to Africa. They've taken me on as a nursing volunteer, I'll be in a hospital first for training, and then I go to Rwanda."

"Oh, Simone!" Sam couldn't say more than that.

"Well, you told me to find some other way, and this is the best way I can find. They need me there, you see, so I'll be useful to someone."

"Do you have to go right away? Before Christmas?"

"Don't stop me, Sam, I really want to go." She paused. "Will you write me? If I write you, will you answer?"

Sam hugged her. "Of course I will. Write me as soon as you get there."

"You'll be the first to hear," said Simone.

She waited till evening, neither patient nor impatient, but in a kind of trance, as though the waiting were part of a necessary ritual. Then she bathed, and dressed, slowly and carefully, like a warrior queen dressing for battle or a woman for her lover, in the red dress and the gold necklace. Then she went out to her car and drove carefully through the streets to his house.

It was only when she got there and saw the upper stories of the house in darkness that she remembered that this was Sunday, and where he would be.

She drove home and sat waiting, knowing that he would not come to her, and yet that he must.

Ben drove with the concentration of a drunk, because one slip would lead him into a maelstrom where he saw nothing but her face. What a fool he had been, thinking that he was safe, thinking that he could make love to her for one night and it would be no worse than if he never did.

He had thought it unbearable before, but now he knew the meaning of that word. It was beyond bearing. He had destroyed himself with that moment of weakness in the night, had burned her forever on his mind and heart and body, and he did not yet know what he had done to her.

He had thought she would see. He had believed, out there in the snow, that if he showed her the truth he would win her. Part of him had known that she might see the truth and still go ahead with the lie, but he had told himself that that was only fear talking.

He drove steadily, trying not to think what his future might hold, how long emptiness had the power to last. Of course he drove to her door, though he had meant to stay away.

She didn't ask who it was when the doorbell rang, because if it was not Ben, it didn't matter who it was. She opened the door and stood waiting for her fate, and whatever it was, she knew she would not run from it again.

He stepped out of the elevator and crossed to her door, and wrapped her in his arms and lifted her, his mouth on hers, and carried her backwards into the apartment, kicking the door shut behind him and leaning against it as his lips, hungry with desperation, devoured her willing mouth.

He had never felt such passion in his life, never known it existed, as if the man who pressed her against him, held her, touched her, kissed her, wrapped her to him, was someone new to him, someone he had never been, had met only when he met her. He lifted his mouth only to murmur broken phrases of love and then kiss her again. It wasn't possible to get enough of her. He would never get enough of her, her face, her hair, her breasts, her body, her soul.

At last, he put his hands up to cup her face, and held it away where he could look at it. "Yes?" he said, knowing he hadn't meant for this to happen. He had meant to talk to her, to make his demands. But he was beyond all demands but one now. Words would come later. Now there was only this.

"Yes," she breathed, and then he bent and swung her up into his arms, and carried her into the darkened bedroom.

13

The red dress fell to the floor under his touch, and then she stood there in all her barbaric splendour, her breasts high and full beneath the heavy gold of the necklace, her thick massed hair flowing down over white shoulders, her eyes dark with female passion, her face more beautiful than any work of art he had ever seen.

He knelt to strip the stockings off her long legs, and then pressed his mouth against the delicate lace of her panties, and with satisfaction heard her gasp. He stood again, and pulled her body to his, lifting her so that she wrapped her legs around his waist. His sex throbbed against her, demanding entry to its natural home, and he laid her down on the bed and kissed her, his mouth as hungry as if he had never kissed her before.

He stood in lamplight and stripped off his clothes as she watched, and when his shorts came off she closed her eyes against the sight of that hungry arousal and what it did to her.

But he would have more control tonight, he told himself, and he drew her body to the edge of the bed, her legs down to the floor, and carefully stripped her briefs off, revealing her moist centre to his eyes, his hands, his mouth. He knelt again, and then she felt the wet fire of his tongue, and her head fell back against the coverlet as she cried out with the pleasure it gave her.

He monitored that pleasure with hands that gripped her hips, felt the tension, the shuddering, heard the uncontrollable cries, and his animal brain whispered that so long as he could do this to her, she could only be his, she could never belong to another man.

She was sobbing with more pleasure than she'd thought was in the world when at last he rose over her again, lifted her bodily onto the bed, and thrust inside with a stroke that shivered through every nerve and cell and out into the room, so that her pleasure, and his, crackled around them.

Then he stopped there, resting on his elbows, deep inside, home, and, looking down at her, waited until her eyes focused on his dark, passion-scarred face.

"Sam," he said. "I love you."

And then, as though those words, which he had never said to any woman, unleashed intolerable feeling in him, he began to thrust into her uncontrollably, wanting her to feel what he felt, wanting to drive everything else out of her mind, everything except that he loved her and she must be his.

Sam's heart jumped painfully in answer, summoning all her blood to her soul's centre, so that she nearly blacked out. "Ben," she whispered from a great distance, floating away from her body and yet tied to the pleasure it gave her. "Ben, Ben, *Ben!*"

"I love you," he told her hoarsely, over and over, as he thrust into her, beyond himself, beyond control, beyond anything except the sound of her wild pleasure and the desperate need to hear what he knew she could not say. "I want you to love me, Sam, say you love me, say you'll try to love me, tell me this is special for you...."

The words and the passion and the wild bursting pleasure had driven her into another world, where they met in another form at the altar she had visited before. "Ben," she said, "I love you, I love you, I've always loved you...."

She heard the high, keening cry of triumph and surrender for a second before her own voice lifted to mingle with it, in the song of oneness and joy that is the central music of the universe.

"Do you love me?" she asked softly, in the perfect silence that came after, wondering what Ben meant by love, and how often he had said those words.

Ben lifted himself on an elbow and smiled down at her. "Haven't I been telling you so for weeks?"

"For *weeks?*"

He watched her quizzically, his dark eyes full of a light she had never seen there. "What did you think it was all about?"

"I thought you—I knew you were attracted to me, but I thought—well, you're not the marrying kind, are you?"

"Is that a gentle way of telling me something?" he asked. His hand clasped her hip. "You will marry me in the end, Sam. I can't let you go now. Whatever security you think Justin and his family's millions can give you, it's not real. I was going to let you go, let you find your security in money if that was what you wanted. But he can't give you what you really need, Sam. If you marry him there'll be nothing but misery, in spite of the money. You'll always be looking for something else."

"You were..." She frowned. "What do you mean, I'll marry you in the end? Is that—"

"Sam," he breathed. "And all this time I thought you knew."

"Thought I knew what?"

"That I love you and want to marry you. You didn't know?"

She swallowed. "But Miranda said...I just assumed that..."

"My mother should be horsewhipped," he said softly. "Didn't it ever occur to you that I'm not married because I've never been in love?"

"No. I thought you were—I thought you wanted me but because I was engaged you were—I mean, until last night I thought it was no more than what you felt for any woman, and that you were trying not to pressure me because of Justin."

He let out a noise half of laughter, half of pain. "I've never been so tortured in my life as I have been over you. You seemed determined to marry Justin at any cost."

"I thought—I thought I loved him. I can see now that you're right, I was blinded by the thought of the security, but I really believed I did."

He took that in in silence for a moment. "And you don't?"

She shook her head. "I saw it all last night. I knew I couldn't marry him, feeling about you the way I did. I knew it must mean you were right, that I didn't love him enough. And I saw that—even if you only wanted me for a week or a month—I couldn't marry him."

He digested what that meant in silence. She had given up all her promise of security for the sake of what might be only a month with him. "As it chances,

I want you for a lifetime," he said roughly. "When are you going to give him back his ring?"

Her dark eyelashes dropped to fan her cheeks, so that he had to kiss her again. "I did that this morning. That's why I had to get back so quickly. So I could tell Justin."

Something went out of his face finally: the dark tension. He stroked her, firmly, as if now, at last, she was really his. "Last night, I walked out in the snow and I came to the decision that, in spite of your determination, if I made love to you, I'd have some chance, I might be able to show you what we had together, and prove to you that marrying Justin wasn't worth it."

"Yes," she said. "It was after we made love that I—" She took a deep breath. "I dreamt we got married, and it was all perfect and right because I loved you. When I woke up I knew it wasn't a dream. I loved you. It wasn't just . . . physical attraction, the way I'd been telling myself."

"Marry me, Sam," he pleaded softly. "Marry me."

"Yes." She laughed in delight.

In the morning Sam added all her new pens to the pot of flowers. "Speaking of birthday gifts," she said, pouring Ben another cup of coffee, "that necklace has what Marie confidently says is a hallmark."

"Does it?"

"Marie says it's solid gold."

"Does she?"

"I didn't believe her. Is it?"

He raised his eyebrows at her.

"You lied to me."

"You were going to refuse the gift."

"Were you going to say something that night?"

"I did say something that night, as I recall. You were adamant."

"Ben, were you—did you buy that to try to prove that you—did you think I'd change my mind if you could show me you could afford…" Her voice faded.

"I bought it because I love you and I was missing you and that necklace reminded me of you."

She smiled and turned to look out at the fresh crop of snow the night had left.

"And speaking of gold, we'll go and get your ring this morning. I know a very good jeweller."

"I've got some paper clips in my desk," she offered.

"I'm sure you do. But as it happens, we won't need one. He'll be open by nine-thirty, and I won't be letting you out of my sight before then."

"Oh, gosh, here?" Sam exclaimed in faint alarm as Ben led her to a doorway she knew well.

"It's a very good jeweller," Ben said. "What's wrong?"

She bit her lip against laughter. "Well, it's where Justin got my ring," she told him. "He's bound to remember me, we were in there so often."

"Oh, well, I suppose he knows a woman's entitled to change her mind," Ben said, and led her inside.

"Morning, Mr. Patel," he said, and the jeweller smiled at them both.

"Mr. Harris," he said. "What can I do for you this fine morning?" Then he looked at Sam again, and his smile broadened almost imperceptibly. "Ah," he said.

"We'd like to look at some rings."

"Engagement rings?" the jeweller asked as though the idea pleased him above and beyond the fact that he was going to make a sale. Sam could feel herself blushing, and hoped it wasn't visible.

A tray of rings came out, and Sam lost her embarrassment in the enchantment of the exotic colours and designs. "Do you really want me to have something like this?" she breathed. There was an Oriental mix of stones, rubies, emeralds, sapphires, diamonds and topazes in rich red gold.

"Only if you like them."

"Oh, I do!"

"This is twenty-two carat gold, a very nice colour," said Mr. Patel, as she drew out a ring composed of a large ruby, two small diamonds and an emerald. "This one I made myself."

They were all beautiful, and she took her time, looking at them all, before deciding on the one that had caught her eye from the first, a large, dark, oval emerald surrounded with tiny diamonds.

"The colour of your eyes, Miss," said Mr. Patel. "It suits you very well, if you will allow me to say so. A very, very good choice, this time, Miss. An excellent choice."

She smiled at him, understanding the message in that. "Yes," said Sam. "I've got it right this time."

And then it was Christmas, with the frozen lake sparkling under the bright sun.

"Cold, isn't it?" Ezra commented, as they strode across the lake. She had collected him at the airport last night, and they had driven up together this morning, Christmas Eve. "Long time since I felt weather like this."

"Kind of like an Alberta winter," Sam agreed. "But you'll love the cottage, Ezra, it's so homelike and cosy."

Ahead of her she saw Ben coming down onto the dock. He stood in the sun for a moment, waving, before he stepped down onto the ice and set out to meet them.

She could see that they liked each other immediately, Ben and Ezra, in that mysterious way of instant man-to-man appraisal, that nod of recognition that here was another man. They chatted easily together, trooping onto the dock and up to the verandah, and then the door was thrust open, and the warmth and family greeting enclosed them all.

"Merry Christmas!" and everyone was kissing and calling and urging coats and boots off and shepherding them into the kitchen, where there was a rich, welcome smell of baking.

"Oh, isn't it beautiful!" Miranda said, grabbing her hand to look at the ring as Sam's gloves came off. "Oh, and I've never realized before that your eyes are exactly emerald."

Ella kissed her. "We're very glad, all of us," she said softly, as Carol and the others also crowded around. And then, in her ear, "You've made the right decision, Sam."

"I know," Sam said thankfully. "I know."

"We're so glad you could come, Ezra," Miranda said later, settling down to talk to her "new daughter's brother" in a quiet corner. "Everything has just worked out so well, don't you agree? Ben and Sam engaged—I found her for him, you know, but for a while there I have to admit I was afraid it wasn't going to go right."

"You did very well," Ezra said amiably, smiling at her in amusement. "I'm glad to see Sam settling into such a happy family."

"Oh, yes, we're just as right for her as she is for us," Miranda agreed. "We're all so happy about it. Ben nearly missed out, you know. Did you know?"

"I knew she'd got herself engaged to Justin," Ezra said.

"Yes, we found her just in time, really."

"I think so." Ezra and Andy exchanged glances that said all they ever needed to say about Justin Mc-Court.

Then Miranda smiled broadly and moved on to new business. "Now, Ezra," she said, "did I understand Sam to say that you haven't got anybody special yourself? Because I know a very nice girl...."

Out in the snow-covered forest, Ben walked with Sam.

"I want to marry you soon. We met at Thanksgiving, got engaged at Christmas, what about a wedding on New Year's Day?"

She turned astonished eyes to him. "Oh, Ben, so fast? Won't we—how would we arrange everything in time? Your mother's already said..."

"I can imagine what she's planning. Would you mind a big wedding, Sam? When I think of it, I'd kind of like it. I don't mind showing you off to the world. It was hard enough to get you."

She smiled and felt all the security of his arm around her. "I'd like a real wedding," she confided softly. "In a church, and Ezra giving me away."

"How about Valentine's Day, then? It'll make them all happy, Andy particularly, and I guess she has a right to her triumph." He laughed, because he *could* laugh now. "I don't know how she found you, but whenever she's most irritating in future, I'll have to remember that she did."

Sam grinned with the secret, and he raised his eyebrows at her. "We'll have to tell you about that, one day," she said. "How Miranda found me."

*   *   *   *   *

Silhouette
Yours Truly has a brand-new look!

Beginning in January 1997, Yours Truly will be sporting a brand-new look. Be sure to look for us as we continue to bring you fabulous stories to carry you into the New Year with a smile on your face:

ME? MARRY YOU?
by Lori Herter

HEIRESS SEEKING PERFECT HUSBAND
by Maris Soule

Truly fun and contemporary, Yours Truly is filled with stories you don't want to miss!

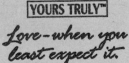

Love—when you least expect it.

Available this January, wherever retail books are sold.

MILLION DOLLAR SWEEPSTAKES

As seen on TV!
Free Gift Offer

With a Free Gift proof-of-purchase from any Silhouette® book,
you can receive a beautiful cubic zirconia pendant.

This gorgeous marquise-shaped stone is a genuine cubic
zirconia—accented by an 18" gold tone necklace.

(Approximate retail value $19.95)

Send for yours today...
compliments of ▼ *Silhouette*®

To receive your free gift, a cubic zirconia pendant, send us one original proof-of-purchase, photocopies not accepted, from the back of any Silhouette Romance™, Silhouette Desire®, Silhouette Special Edition®, Silhouette Intimate Moments® or Silhouette Yours Truly™ title available in August, September, October, November and December at your favorite retail outlet, together with the Free Gift Certificate, plus a check or money order for $1.65 U.S./$2.15 CAN. (do not send cash) to cover postage and handling, payable to Silhouette Free Gift Offer. We will send you the specified gift. Allow 6 to 8 weeks for delivery. Offer good until December 31, 1996 or while quantities last. Offer valid in the U.S. and Canada only.

Free Gift Certificate

Name: _____

Address: _____

City: _____ State/Province: _____ Zip/Postal Code: _____

Mail this certificate, one proof-of-purchase and a check or money order for postage and handling to: SILHOUETTE FREE GIFT OFFER 1996. In the U.S.: 3010 Walden Avenue, P.O. Box 9077, Buffalo NY 14269-9077. In Canada: P.O. Box 613, Fort Erie, Ontario L2Z 5X3.

FREE GIFT OFFER   084-KMD
ONE PROOF-OF-PURCHASE
To collect your fabulous FREE GIFT, a cubic zirconia pendant, you must include this original proof-of-purchase for each gift with the properly completed Free Gift Certificate.

084-KMD-R

HOW MUCH IS THAT COUPLE IN THE WINDOW?
by Lori Herter

Book 1 of Lori's Million-Dollar Marriages miniseries
Yours Truly™—February

Salesclerk Jennifer Westgate's new job is to live in a department store display window for a week as the bride of a gorgeous groom. Here's what sidewalk shoppers have to say about them:

"Why is the window so steamy tonight? I can't see what they're doing!"
—Henrietta, age 82

"That mousey bride is hardly Charles Derring's type. It's me who should be living in the window with him!"
—Delphine, Charles's soon-to-be ex-girlfriend

"Jennifer never modeled pink silk teddies for me! This is an outrage!"
—Peter, Jennifer's soon-to-be ex-boyfriend

"How much is that couple in the window?"
—Timmy, age 9

HOW MUCH IS THAT COUPLE IN THE WINDOW?
by Lori Herter—Book 1 of her Million-Dollar Marriages miniseries—available in February from

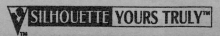

SILHOUETTE YOURS TRULY™

Love—when you least expect it!

LHMILLION

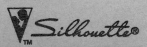